UNMASK

CALENTHIA YVETTE MILLER

S.H.E. PUBLISHING, LLC

llustration by Anthony L. Wardrett

Worldloveart@gmail.com

Instagram @worldloveart

For information contact:
info@shepublishingllc.com
www.shepublishingllc.com
T : 219.515.8032

Book Cover and Title Page design by Michelle Phillips of

CHELLD3 3D VISUALIZATION AND DESIGN

ISBN:

978-1-953163-54-7 (paperback)
978-1-953163-55-4 (hardback)

First Edition: December 2022

10 9 8 7 6 5 4 3 2 1

CONTENTS

$\mathcal{D}$EDICATION

I dedicate this book to my boys, Lorenzo and Kahari. We have seen our fair share of heartache, turmoil, and missteps, but through it all, we have an unbreakable bond sealed with love. Thank you for being a part of this journey and allowing me to be your mother, mentor, protector, prayer warrior, and friend. To my dad, Leon Sr.; Clarence; my brother, Leon Jr.; my mother, Calenthia; my sister, Patrice; my nephews, Marcell, Kevin, Solomon, Langston, and Braxton; my grand- daughter, Armoni; and my extended family and friends. Thank you for the continuous prayers, support, and well wishes. You all have played a pivotal part in my recovery. However, there is not enough gratitude or thanks, as my life belongs to my Father in Heaven. He has allowed me to share my gift with you. He saw the potential when I did not, restoring me when I was lost and broken. For this, Lord, I give you praise.

"Be strong and courageous. Do not be afraid or terrified because of them, for the Lord your God goes with you; he will never leave you or forsake you." (Deuteronomy 31:6)

Love,

Calenthia

$\mathcal{P}$ROLOGUE

Anya had come to realize that the one thing she looked forward to after a long day at work was the one thing she had come to dread, which was a peaceful night of sleep. For the past three months, Anya had been having these reoccurring dreams that she could not figure out. Her night routine for over two decades was listening to slow jams while submerging herself in a luxurious, hot bath. The steam from the tub was what relaxed her mind, caressed her aching muscles, and washed away the events of the day. But the glass of Moscato and scented candles were what set the mood. As far back as she could remember, her sense of curiosity and childlike spirit were what allowed her to survive over the years. Anya longed to escape to faraway destinations, adventures, and fantasies where only her mind could take her. This all changed on January 20, when the life she once knew was no more, and the dreams began.

Thursday, January 20, was a typical day, with meetings back-to-back and phones ringing off the hook. She was running several reports in preparation for an upcoming national leadership conference and waiting on a large supply shipment that had been delayed due to COVID restrictions. Nothing that day or even earlier in the week stood out that would give Anya a reason to be concerned. Around midday, Anya stopped to speak with the team as she always did. The conversation was light and upbeat as everyone looked forward to the upcoming weekend. As Anya exited the common area on the way back to her office, she was approached by Leah.

Leah Bernard had been employed with the company for about seven years; she was straightforward and did not hesitate to speak her mind. Anya and Leah shared a special relationship that allowed them to always keep it real with one another. When Anya decided to relocate and open her consulting firm, the first person she thought of was Leah. Although Leah was a little rough around the edges, she was loyal and a hard worker. Over the years, their bond had blossomed into a sisterhood.

Leah said, "Boss lady, is everything all right? You have not been yourself all week."

"Yes, all is good. It's been hectic, and I have a lot on my plate, but nothing I cannot handle."

As they entered Anya's office, she immediately reached for her water and the Aleve. Leah looked up from the chair where she was sitting and said, "You need a vacation, like yesterday."

Anya laughed and replied, "Miami does sound good right about now."

The concern in Leah's eyes showed that she genuinely cared. She stood to leave, and before exiting, she said to Anya, "I am concerned you have been burning the candle at both ends; please stop and take care of yourself."

Anya began to reflect on what Leah had said. *I could use a few days for myself, and a nice getaway would be refreshing.* Anya had not taken a proper vacation since opening the business nearly eight years before. Her last trip to Miami had been about three years before with a few friends. The time spent there was magnificent. The people were lovely, and the food was sinful. She could still feel the warm ocean breeze sweeping across her face while relaxing on the deck of the oceanside villa. She made a mental note to have Stacie, her secretary, begin clearing her calendar and looking for a flight. Maybe Leah was right. A vacation was just what she needed.

CHAPTER 1

FLASH WARNING

Anya peered up at the flashing red numbers on her alarm clock; she prayed that her eyes were playing a cruel trick on her. Unfortunately, this could not be correct because she had just closed her eyes at 4:27 a.m., and it was now 6:00 a.m. She had tossed and turned all night long; to make matters worse, the air conditioner had stopped working sometime during the middle of the night. Anya contemplated taking a personal day because she was so exhausted. Deciding against that idea, she reached for her cell phone and texted Stacie so she could switch the day's first meeting to a conference call, and she would be in by ten.

Willing herself to get up, Anya stumbled out of bed and headed to the bathroom. Once there, she glared at the reflection in the mirror. Anya immediately became sad as she did not recognize the person staring back at her. The once-vibrant woman had been replaced by a worn-down individual who was twenty pounds lighter, with dark circles under her eyes and a headache that had been relentless for the past three days. Anya thought this must be what it felt like to have a hangover from partying all night. Mustering up everything in her, she showered, got dressed, and retrieved two Aleve and all the necessary items she needed for work. Anya said a small prayer, as she always did before heading out to start her day.

The sun began to shine down from the heavens, making way for another hot and humid day. Anya made her way down the crowded sidewalk toward her favorite coffee shop to pick up a large vanilla bean Frappuccino with 2 percent milk, whipped cream, and caramel drizzle. The anticipation of the savory concoction was just what Anya needed after yet another sleepless night. As she approached the coffee shop, her phone began to vibrate; she looked at the number and quickly answered it. The rich, baritone voice on the other end brought a smile and an instant chill to her body, even though it was hot outside.

Anya had been communicating with Royce Blackmon for nearly a year. Royce had been referred to her by one of the company's loyal clients and a friend, Abbey Winstead. Abbey and Anya had met at a women's empowerment retreat in Chicago about five years before. They were seated at the same table during the event, and at one of the breakout sessions, Anya and Abbey were asked to partner on a project. They quickly realized that they had so much in common. They both shared a philanthropic spirit. And giving back to the community they served drove them to succeed. Since then, they had forged a great business and personal relationship. Last month, they had worked together on a mentorship program that provided young entrepreneurs with the necessary resources and tools to assist them in growing their businesses.

"Good morning, Ms. McMichael. I hope that your day is going well thus far. Are you available to talk?"

Anya smiled and said, "Sure, how may I help you this fine morning?"

Royce chuckled. "If only you knew."

Anya was not sure how she should respond. The only interaction she had had with Mr. Blackmon was their phone conversations. He could walk right by or stand behind her in this line. She had no clue what he looked like, but if he sounded like his voice, he must be sexy and smell exquisite. She quickly regained her composure and played it safe and responded professionally.

"Yes, I can talk, Mr. Blackmon."

"Great, did you receive my last spreadsheet?"

"Yes, I received your spreadsheet, and based on the numbers, it looks like you will need to add about five additional support personnel to your team if you want to see your forecasted numbers by the end of the fiscal year. In addition, the salary and benefits package you are proposing is not in range with the current market. You are way too low and will be beaten out by a more seasoned company willing to pay their candidates top dollar based on their knowledge and skills. Consider offering a more enticing benefits package to offset the pay."

She could hear Mr. Blackmon take a long breath, followed by a period of silence.

"Well, Ms. McMichael, I believe that I have taken up way too much of your time. Nevertheless, I will consider your suggestion. Have a great rest of your day."

Before she could respond, the line had disconnected. Anya was unsure if she should be upset because of his rudeness or delighted that he would consider her suggestions. Whether Mr. Blackmon took the necessary actions or not, she was secure and confident in what she had conveyed, and it would be his decision in the end. She placed her order and waited for her number to be called.

Anya retrieved her Frappuccino and a coffee cake that she did not need. She headed out of the shop to take the short thirty-minute stroll to her office. She quickly regretted her decision to walk; it had not been ten minutes, and the sweat began trickling down her back. She was perplexed; had the temperature changed since leaving the house? She checked the weather on her phone; it showed the current temperature was seventy-three degrees with a 20 percent chance of rain by noon.

She took a long sip of her drink, hoping that this would cool her off. Then, without any warning, her head began to pound, and a wave of nausea came over her like a tsunami crashing into the shores of a secluded beach. She quickly surveyed the area and noticed that she was only a few steps from the park, which meant she was in close proximity to her office building. She went to a nearby bench and sat down, placing her head in her hands. She was not sure which hurt more, her head or stomach. She remembered not taking the pain medication before leaving the house. She rambled through her purse to retrieve the pill bottle and some ginger chews to relieve her nausea. She sat until she felt a sense of relief returning. She slowly began to stand, praying that she would not faint. The first steps proved to be a bit of a task, as she was very unstable on her feet. She opted to sit back down and not risk falling and causing additional injuries. She remained sitting for what seemed like an eternity. The headache and nausea had not let up, so she decided to call Stacie and have her cancel all her meetings for the day. Minutes later, an Uber arrived to take her home.

The commute from the park was longer than anticipated because of an earlier accident. However, she welcomed the time as it allowed the medication to take effect and slowly reduce the unbearable pain in her head. The driver apologized for the traffic and asked if she was ok. Anya slowly opened her eyes and indicated that she had a terrible headache. He advised that he had suffered from migraines in the past, and the headaches went away once he reduced his caffeine intake and changed his diet. He offered her the name of his neurologist and suggested that she give him a call. Anya asked him his name, and he said, "Gerald." She was grateful for his concern and took the paper with the name and number. They arrived at her residence less than ten minutes later. Gerald assisted her out of the vehicle.

Anya again thanked him for his generosity and for referring her to his physician. Gerald waited until she was safely inside before driving off. Anya took the short ride to the top floor of the newly renovated converted brewery in the heart of Brentwood. The elevator opened to a private entrance to her unit. She quickly removed her shoes, laid her belongings on the console, and headed to the oversized sectional in the living room. Anya slowly eased her head against the couch cushions, praying that she did not make any sudden movements that would cause the headache to intensify. She closed her weary eyes, and before she knew it, she was fast asleep.

CHAPTER 2

BY CHANCE

Anya awoke to the sounds of loud banging and what she thought to be shattering glass. She looked around, and the living room was completely dark. It had still been light outside when she had arrived home from the park. She slowly turned and lifted her head toward the sound of her phone vibrating, indicating that she had a missed call. She reached out and grabbed the device and noticed that she had thirty-two missed calls and a slew of text messages. The last text was from Leah at 10:17 p.m. The message read:

I have been blowing up your phone and leaving messages for ten hours. Where are you? If I don't get a return call in an hour, I will call the police.

She looked at the time, and it was 12:47 a.m. She dialed Leah's number and ran toward the banging noise. She quickly stopped when she saw the doorknob turn. She retreated to her bedroom, opened the nightstand drawer, and grabbed Lou. Lou was her pink Glock 43X 9mm pistol. She had purchased her shortly after she had relocated to Brentwood. As a single, attractive female in an urban area, she needed something that would give her peace of mind, especially since a dog was not an option. As she proceeded back down the hallway toward the door, she vaguely heard a woman's voice. The voice sounded familiar but distorted.

Her adrenaline was overloaded, and she had forgotten that she had called Leah before entering her bedroom. She pulled the phone from her pocket and quietly spoke into the receiver: "Hey, Leah, I am OK, but I think someone is at my door trying to break in. I got Lou, and I am headed back down the hallway."

Leah quickly responded, "Anya, I called the police, and they are probably at the door doing a welfare check."

"Hold on; I have another call from an unknown number coming in on the other line." Typically, Anya would not have answered it, but she clicked over, and was greeted by a male who introduced himself as Dispatcher Donovan, and he was calling from the Brentwood 911 Emergency Call Center. He asked her name and if there was anyone else in the home besides herself. She provided him with her name and advised him that no one else was in the house. He said they had received several calls from friends and family concerned about her well-being that night.

"Ms. McMichael, there is an officer at the door named Sergeant Collins. Can you please go and open the door for him? I will stay on the line until you do."

Anyacould hear someone talking as she approached the door: "We have contacted the home's resident, and she is headed your way."

She turned the doorknob and opened the door, and much to her surprise, a large muscular male figure stood there. He slowly turned around, and she nearly passed out.

"Hello, Ms. McMichael. I am Sergeant Collins, with the Brentwood Police Department. As Dispatcher Donovan has advised, we have received several calls tonight requesting a welfare check. Is everything OK?"

She felt as if the room had begun to spin, and everything went black before she could utter another word.

Anya could hear someone calling her name; the voice sounded as if it was coming from a long distance; they continued to call her name several times. Then she felt someone gently squeezing her hand and stroke her head. Their touch reminded her of when she was sick as a child and how her mom would rock her in her arms while singing softly in her ear until she fell into a deep, peaceful sleep. Then, the voice began to get louder and closer. She slowly opened her eyes and was immediately met with the most piercing grayish-blue eyes she had ever seen. She continued to stare, as she was captivated not only by the eyes but the fullness of the beautiful lips.

"Ms. McMichael, it's Sergeant Collins. You passed out. I called the EMTs, and they are on the way."

She scanned her surroundings and saw that she was on the

couch. The last thing she remembered was opening the door, and then everything had gone dark.

Sergeant Collins must have seen the confusion and fear in her eyes. He responded, "You opened the door, and that's when you went down; I immediately brought you in and placed you on the couch for some privacy."

All Anya could hear was the word "*privacy.*" Why had he used that word? Sergeant Collins pointed his finger toward the upper half of her torso as he turned his body slightly in the chair. Her brain was racing into overdrive, and she felt her face flush. She peeked under the throw that she kept on the back of the sectional. She had no shirt on, only her lace bra. It made sense she had removed her shirt, because the air conditioning had stopped working two nights before. She needed to call the warranty company ASAP.

"Your friend Leah is downstairs waiting on the ambulance to arrive. She worried when you didn't return her call after speaking with dispatch."

She noticed that Sergeant Collins had not released her hand. His grip seemed tighter, but the gentle way he held her hand did not change; at that moment, she felt safe.

"Ms. McMichael, I can give you some privacy so you can put on your shirt before the medics arrive."

She nodded her head, and he released her hand. He stood and walked toward the floor-to-ceiling window while she dressed.

Anya must have fallen asleep for a few minutes because she did not feel as tired as before. She looked up, and Sergeant Collins was gone. She suddenly panicked, and her heart began to race. What had happened? Had he been dispatched to another call, and would she see him again? As she began to stand, she felt a familiar touch on her back above her hip.

He whispered, "Please sit; the crew is on the way, and I don't want you to hurt yourself."

The coolness of his breath against her ear made her knees go weak. What was it about him that made her lose all sense of reality? She turned to face him. Just as their eyes locked, she could hear the elevator doors open and the gurney wheels making their way across the marble floor down the corridor toward her unit. Before another word could be spoken, the medics came around the corner, and Leah was only a few steps behind them. Within minutes, her living room became Grand Central Station, and she was a passenger waiting to board the train to nowhere.

The medics began to assess her condition. She had one taking her vitals and another asking about her medical history. Her eyes scanned the room for Sergeant Collins. She noticed that he and Leah were talking with another medic. The medic came over to Anya.

"Ms. McMichael, I spoke with Sergeant Collins. He advised that when you passed out, your head struck the cement floor, and he was concerned that you might have a concussion. Also, Ms. Bernard said you have not been feeling well for some time. Therefore, I think we should transport you to the nearest hospital for further testing."

By this time, Leah was standing at the end of the gurney with Anya's purse and keys in her hand. The medic secured the seat belt across her hips, and they were on their way to Coventry Memorial Hospital.

CHAPTER 3

*Un*CERTATIES

nya awoke to the sun peeking out from the slightly drawn curtains. She felt as if she was coming out of a fog. Where was she? This clearly was not her bedroom nor her bed. She went to raise her right hand, and a sharp pain radiated down her arm like a lightning bolt. She grimaced, as she had never experienced pain like that before. After the pain subsided, she managed to push herself up in the bed using her left hand. The events of the night before were unclear. What had happened after leaving her house? Where was Leah? She lay there looking up at the ceiling. Suddenly the memories of the night before began to come back.

Things seemed to go downhill fast once she had agreed to be transported.

When she had arrived and entered the bay doors to the emergency room, panic had set in, and fear had consumed every fiber of her body. She could not pinpoint what was going on. She had been in a hospital many times. Then it hit her that this was the first time she had been in a hospital since her father had passed. The images of him lying in that bed flooded her psyche. She could not turn it off or make it go away. The tears began to fall like the rain on a day in April. Her world was crumbling piece by piece, and she could not do anything to stop or control it.

She knew that she was in a hospital, but had she had a nervous breakdown? Had she been committed? Then she heard something—or someone—move in the corner of the room. A light suddenly came on, which blinded her momentarily. Once her eyes shifted, she saw that Leah was standing in front of her. She looked exhausted, and Anya could tell that she had been crying. Before Anya could ask any questions, Leah said, "Bitch, you scared the shit out of me." Then she gave Anya a big bear hug that took her breath away. Once Leah released her, Anya could not even look her in her eyes. She felt horrible and guilty for putting her through all of this.

Leah knew something was wrong. "Before you say anything, I wanted to be here, and if it had been me in this hospital bed, you would have done the same for me. This is what family does for each other. Now straighten up that damn face before I give you something to cry about."

They both immediately began to laugh.

Leah began to fill her in on some of the things that had transpired over the last three days. What Anya thought had happened in one day had happened in three. Leah said that when she had gotten to the hospital, she was told that Anya had had a panic attack and that they needed to sedate her because they were concerned that she might have a concussion or some other brain injury. Unfortunately, Leah could not provide many details because of the strict privacy laws.

A knock at the door pulled them away from their conversation. A young female entered the room. She said, "I am glad to see that you are awake Ms. McMichael. I am Dr. Lassiter, one of the neurologists who has followed your case since you were admitted. How are you feeling?"

"I am doing OK, I guess."

Dr. Lassiter smiled. "This is confusing and probably overwhelming, but I am here to answer all your questions. Ms. McMichael, we ran a battery of tests over the last few days. A CAT Scan of your head was done…"

Anya braced herself and held Leah's hand for support in anticipation of some bad news.

"You did suffer a concussion, but no other injuries, such as a bleed, were seen in the images. We wanted to keep you sedated in the event that there were. Your labs did show that your magnesium and potassium were low; we had to give them in your IV. So you may experience some pain and burning when it is administered. Now that you are awake, we can discontinue it and have you take it by mouth. The emergency room physician has requested someone from psychiatry to come and speak with you regarding your panic attack. Have you ever had a panic attack before?"

Anya shook her head no.

"Do you have any idea why you had the attack?"

Anya told Dr. Lassiter about her dad's passing and how it related to the hospital. Dr. Lassiter reassured Anya that panic attacks could occur after a traumatic event such as a death. She asked if she had any more questions, and Anya said no. Dr. Lassiter wished her well before leaving. Anya and Leah were very impressed with her and the time she took to address all of Anya's concerns.

Shortly after Dr. Lassiter left, several more physicians came and gave her an update on her condition. Dr. Gonzales, from psychiatry, also suggested that she find a counselor to help her with the trauma of losing her dad. She finally convinced Leah to go home and shower and get some rest before she left; she thanked her for the beautiful flowers she had brought.

Leah said, "I can't take all the credit; they came from the girls at the office, Abbey, and someone name Collins."

C HAPTER 4

PUTTING THINGS IN PERSPECTIVE

oyce Blackmon stood at the window, looking out at the city. He could not concentrate because all his thoughts were on this mysterious woman, Anya McMichael. When Royce had run into Abbey at the charity gala nearly a year before and sparked a conversation regarding his next business venture, she had immediately suggested he contact Anya. Abbey raved about the success she had had since partnering with her. Over his ten-plus years as a lawyer and businessman, he had learned always to do his homework when involving others in his finances.

He knew he could have easily asked Abbey about her but

quickly dismissed the idea. Anya had an imposing resume, starting with working for two top nonprofit organizations, graduating at the top of her class, and earning her doctorate in healthcare administration with an emphasis on leadership. She was also a published author and now a businesswoman. She had recently purchased and renovated a brewery in Brentwood and converted the top floor into her home. She had never married and had no children.

What was it about Anya that intrigued him so much? Royce could have any woman he wanted. But Anya was different from any other woman he had met. She made him think. All the other women he had slept with only wanted one thing, and that was his money. He wanted more than just a bedmate; he wanted a soulmate. He grasped the small locket around his neck, opened the clasp, and looked at the picture of his beloved. Tears filled his eyes. How he missed and longed for her touch.

The phone rang, interrupting his thoughts.

"Hello, this is Royce; how can I help you?"

"Darling, did you miss me?"

Royce instantly wished that he had not answered.

"Are you not going to say anything?"

"Bria, why are you calling me and not your lawyer?"

Bria was a woman who fell into the category of just wanting his money. He had met Bria Gregory two years before. He was leaving the cleaners, and she was coming in. He was talking to the owner and ran right into her. And in doing so, he had caused the coffee she was drinking to get on her blouse and the white pantsuit she had in her hand. He immediately apologized and offered to pay for the cleaning of her garments. He gave her his business card and told her to call him if the stain could not be removed.

About three weeks later, while going through his voicemails, he heard a message: "This is Bria, the lady from the cleaners. Can you give me a call?" He called her the next day, and they agreed to meet that Saturday at the restaurant across the street from the cleaners. Their meeting went well, to say the least. They had a casual fling with no strings attached for about a year and a half.

One evening his boy Lucas called and invited him out to celebrate his upcoming nuptials. Royce agreed to meet him at one of the local bars in the area. Lucas had one too many shots, so Royce decided to drive Lucas's car and come back for his own later. As they were exiting, Royce ran into Bria. He asked if she could follow him in his car while he took Lucas home, and he would take her home afterward. Well, Bria never made it to her house that night. The last time Royce heard from her was six months ago when she said she was pregnant.

Initially, when Bria let him know about the pregnancy, he was shocked. Shit, he was forty-one and had never had a woman tell him she was carrying his baby. The exception to that would be Skylar.

Skylar Monroe was his beloved. They had met when they

were juniors at Coventry Preparatory Academy. Skylar was the new kid on the block, and every dude tried to get at her. Skylar made it very clear that she was all about her studies. Of course, Royce, being Mr. Casanova, had to spit that game to her. He carefully watched all his boys try and strike out. Finally, lady luck waved her magic wand, and he and Skylar had biology together. Mrs. Sullivan, their teacher, announced that they had to partner up for a project that was 50 percent of their grade, and she would post the assigned groups by the end of the week. That was the longest week ever. By the end of the class on Friday, Mrs. Sullivan had posted the assignment, and Skylar was his partner for the next nine weeks. In his mind, he had nine weeks to sweep her off her feet and make her his. Now Skylar Monroe was no pushover, and she was very familiar with who Royce was. The next day in class, Skylar came up to him and handed him a meticulously handwritten agenda of how they would design and complete their project. At the bottom of the paper, Skylar had boldly written:

If You Think That I Am Going To Be Your Next Conquest, You Are Sadly Mistaken Because I Am A Lady And Will Be Treated As Such!

From that day forward, they were inseparable. Skylar taught him the meaning of unconditional love. She was the person to whom he told his secrets, aspirations, goals, and fears. They were each other's first everything. He loved her to the moon and beyond. They dated for the next ten years. Skylar wanted to be established and finish school before getting married. So on March 1, ten years after meeting, they married.

Skylar had landed her dream job at Vanderbilt as a speech

pathologist, and Royce was hired at Woods, King, and Jackson Law Firm right out of school. He was the youngest attorney to make partner in their seventy-five-year history. The night they were celebrating their fifth anniversary, Skylar called and said she would be late and to expect her around 6:00 p.m. at La-Trujillo, their favorite Mexican restaurant, and that she had a surprise for him. He had flown her family in to surprise her. His parents and siblings were in attendance also.

He knew that she would get cases added on now and then. He began to worry when she had not arrived, and it was now 8:00 p.m. He called her cell phone, and it went straight to voicemail. He called her job, and they said she had left around 5:30 p.m. They all decided to leave and meet back at the house. As they left the restaurant, his friend Lucas came in; Royce immediately knew something was wrong. Lucas was a state trooper, and he had said he would not be able to attend the dinner because he had to work.

"Royce, I am so sorry. Skylar was involved in a head-on collision. She is gone, man!"

The funeral was beautiful, but the months that followed were a blur. Royce was a wreck; he did not eat or sleep. He was a shell of the man he once was. How was he supposed to exist in this world without Skylar? One evening while he was sitting in the den where he spent most of the time after the funeral, he received a knock at his front door. When he opened it, there stood an elderly gentleman. Royce asked how he could help him.

The gentleman extended his hand and said, "I am Daniel Overton; I am sorry to bother you, but I used to live here many years ago, and before I left this world, I wanted to visit the place that brought me joy."

Royce invited Mr. Overton in, as it had begun to rain. He offered him something to drink. Mr. Overton took a seat and began to explain that he and his late wife, Elizabeth, had purchased the house when they married back in 1941. Mr. Overton lit up as he told of the times spent there in the house with his children and wife. He bent his head and said, "I was the luckiest man in the world to have been loved by her." Mr. Overton stood and walked the length of the living room. As he got to the fireplace, he said, "It is still here." Royce went to see what he was pointing at.

There beside the mantel was a heart with the initials *D+E; you are why I live.* Royce had never noticed it because it was where his and Skylar's wedding picture hung. He had taken it down because it was too painful to look at daily. Mr. Overton ran his finger over the heart and began to cry. They talked for nearly two hours before he stood to leave. As Mr. Overton descended the stairs, he said, "Whatever you are going through, this too shall pass. Trust in the process; your time to love again is coming."

About a week later, Royce received a certified letter advising that the people in the other car involved in the accident were suing for pain and suffering. They claimed that Skylar was under the influence and at fault. Royce was livid. He knew for a fact that Skylar was not a drinker. She would not even drink sparkling champagne. He distinctly remembered that Skylar had mentioned that she needed to schedule her annual employee screening the week of the accident. He went to the bedroom that they shared. He retrieved the box Lucas had given him a few days after they processed the vehicle. He located the results of her toxicology report, and it was negative.

Then he found an envelope addressed to himself. He opened it, and it was a card. He began to read it:

To My Everything,

You were my first love, protector, soulmate, and soon to be the father of our child.

Folded in the card was a picture of an ultrasound.

It is painful to this day when his reads the note from Skylar. Royce would be the first to admit that he was no saint and was far from perfect. He took full responsibility for his actions and his role in this situation. He knew he had a reputation for being a whore, and that sooner or later, this would come around and bite him in the ass.

Bria began threatening and making harassing calls. The last straw was the vandalism of his home. He had to get a lawyer involved. One night over the phone, Royce and Bria agreed that a paternity test would be done when the child was born, because she was married and seeing someone beside him. He ended the call with Bria and immediately dialed Chris Calloway, his attorney and one of his closest friends. His calls went to voicemail. He had to pull himself together. An unborn child was involved, and he had to do what was best for them. Royce went to his desk and pulled out the ultrasound picture, safely secured in the Bible that he and Skylar had received on their wedding day from his granny. The inscription read:

On this day, you became one. Your union was witnessed in the sight of all who love you. But it was created by Our Father in Heaven. Make no mistake; you will have trials and tribulations on this journey. Your love will be tested. And you will have to put in overtime to make it work. But always remember why you committed yourself to one another. Make each other your priority as God does us. Keep His word as your foundation, as He is the creator of what is good in all of us.

Love Granny,

Mariam Bell-Blackmon

Royce cried out in agony: "I SHOULD BE HAVING A BABY WITH MY WIFE!"

CHAPTER 5

*In*SECURITIES

Sgt. Sebastián Collins contemplated whether to reach out to Anya. It had been a month since he had seen her. On the night of the call, he had been headed home only two blocks from Anya's house. He radioed dispatch to let them know he could head that way if they didn't have an available unit. Her disheveled hair framed her beautiful, round, caramel face when she opened the door. Her brown eyes had a hue of gray that danced in the light that hung from the ceiling over her door. And what could he say about the black lace bra other than *"Damn!"*

Why did he feel compelled to try to save her? Was it a sense of duty to ensure that she was protected? Sebastián did not want to overstep his boundaries, especially since he had no idea if she was in a relationship. And he had witnessed her having a panic attack.

He was no stranger to mood swings and psychotic episodes. He had a family history of mental illness. His mother had been diagnosed with depression shortly before he turned ten; as a young child coming home without food, lights, or running water, he had been scared, not knowing where his mom was for days.

His mom was terrific if she took her medication. There was one afternoon he would never forget. He had to have been about eight, and they lived in a three-bedroom apartment in the suburbs of Chattanooga. His mom worked as a realtor, and her hours were never the same weekly. When she worked late, Sebastián would go to their neighbors, Mr. and Mrs. Franklin. The Franklins were the grandparents he never had, because his had died when his mom had been a teenager.

The school bus pulled up to the front of the apartment, and typically, if his mom did not work late, she would be there to greet him. On this day, Mrs. Franklin was there to retrieve him. He exited the bus and waved "bye" to the driver.

Mrs. Franklin said, "Sebastián, how was your day at school?"

He replied that it was not too bad; he was just glad it was the weekend. "Where's Mom? Did she have to work late again?"

"Yes, she called and asked that I pick you up from the bus. She said she should be home around 7:00 p.m. I guess it will be me, you, and Pop Franklin tonight."

They made their way up the walkway to Mrs. Franklin's apartment. They entered the door, and the aroma of the fried chicken hit him as soon as he crossed the threshold. Pop Franklin was standing in front of the stove with a towel draped across his shoulder. He was swaying to the music that came from the radio that sat on the table.

He said, "Young man, what do you know about that kind of music?" He grabbed Mrs. Franklin's hand, and they began to dance. He looked deeply into her eyes as if no one or nothing else existed. He kissed her on her forehead, and she kissed him back. Before they released one another, they both said, "I love you."

Sebastián laid his belongings on the chair next to the door. Mrs. Franklin said dinner would be ready to serve in an hour.

"Do you want a snack?"

Sebastián nodded yes. She went to the cabinet and pulled out a package of Lorna Doone cookies. She looked in the fridge and said, "Sweetie, we need some milk."

"OK, Sebastián and I can go and get some." Sebastián and Pop Franklin left the apartment en route to the store. As he was a young boy with no father or mentor, their time spent together talking meant the world to Sebastián.

They returned with the milk, and Mrs. Franklin had the table set. There was fried chicken, macaroni and cheese, broccoli, homemade rolls, and freshly squeezed lemonade. After eating, Sebastián helped clear and wash the dishes. He looked at the clock over the sink, and it was 6:50 p.m. Mom should be there to get him in ten minutes.

Well, that ten minutes turned into two days. Over the next few years, Mom's appearance began to change, and she became withdrawn. Then she lost her job. It was precisely two days before he had turned ten when he came home from school and the police and ambulance were parked in front of their building. Sebastián became anxious because the week before, Mom had been missing. *Is she back? Is she ok?* Then he thought, *Has something happened to Pop. and Ma. Franklin?* He ran toward the building as Pop Franklin came out the entry door.

Pop said, "Sebastián, let's take a ride; we need to get some milk from the store."

Sebastián got in the front seat of the car. They headed out of the parking garage toward the store. But Pop turned onto the street near the park about a mile from the house.

Pop said, "You know I would never lie to you."

Sebastián said, "Yes, I know."

"You know that Ja'Nae has not been doing well these last few years." (Ja'Nae was his mom's first name.)

Sebastián said yes.

"She must go somewhere to get help and has asked us to look after you until she returns." Sebastián immediately began to sob uncontrollably. Pop reached over, scooped him up in his arms, and said, "I love you as if you were my own. I will fight until my dying day to make sure you are safe."

Pop and Ma Franklin became his adoptive parents, and

from that day on, he had not seen or spoken to his mom, Ja'Nae.

He was thirty-eight years old, had never married, and had one child, and he still suffered from abandonment issues. However, Ma and Pop Franklin were the best things that had ever happened to him. They had taken excellent care of him. Pop Franklin molded him into the man that he was today.

Ma Franklin still hoped that Ja'Nae and Sebastián could repair their relationship. He'd tell her, "I am not opposed to exploring a relationship with her. However, my top priority is Ocean."

Ocean was his fifteen-year-old daughter, whom he coparented with his ex-girlfriend Marisa. Every time he looked at Ocean, he realized how important it was to be present in her life. Sebastián pulled out the key to his Kawasaki Ninja 650R and placed his helmet on for safety; he needed to go to his quiet spot to think.

$\mathcal{C}$HAPTER 6

ROAD TO RECOVERY

Anya eased her head off the goose-down pillows that framed her head. She slipped her feet into her slippers and headed to the bathroom to shower and brush her teeth. It had been a month since she had been released from the hospital, and she had not returned to work, but she had made it a point to schedule time to see a therapist and the neurologist that Gerald had referred her to.

Anya had not experienced any headaches or nausea like before. But she did start having a reoccurring dream of a child. Anya knew she was not pregnant, because she had not been sexually active since being with Grayson, a relationship which had ended over seven months before.

She made her way to the kitchen to prepare breakfast and water her plants, which desperately needed it. Anya began to smile as she looked at the vase of yellow roses and thought of Sergeant Collins. Anya smiled as she remembers reading the cards inserted in the flowers from the hospital. When she got the flowers from him, her hands began to shake as she remembered his touch. She took in a deep breath and read the card:

Ms. McMichael,

I hope you are on the road to a speedy recovery, and these yellow roses will brighten your day.

Sebastián Collins

Anya wanted to contact Sebastián to thank him for the beautiful roses, but she had no way of doing so. She could go to the police station, but she had no idea which station he worked at. Honestly, she was scared and did not want to set herself up for disappointment. Anya remembered what Eileen, her therapist, had said: "Not facing your fears head on causes undue stress and turmoil." Eileen had suggested that Anya begin journaling and constructing a vision board.

Anya decided that she would go out today and purchase the materials for the board and a journal. But first, she needed to clean this house. The last thing she had thought of when she had returned home was cleaning. She finished watering the plants, ate breakfast, and headed to the living room to start. Her phone rang, and it was Abbey. The last time they had spoken was two days after she had gotten home from the hospital. Anya was happy to hear her voice.

Although Anya was the older of the two, Abbey always gave the vibe that she was. Abbey wanted a rundown of everything Anya had been doing since arriving home. Anya gave Abbey the condensed version, and she was OK with it.

She emphasized that she had not been to work or looked at anything work related. That made Abbey happy. They chatted for another thirty minutes, and just before the call ended, Abbey said that the annual Minority Leadership and Entrepreneurship Gala was taking place in two weeks. The keynote speakers were Justice Ketanji Brown-Jackson and Senator Corey Booker; would she be interested in going?

Anya said without hesitation, "Hell yeah, girl; I'm in!" Abbey gave her the details, and they said their goodbyes.

> **Sgt. Sebastián Collins**
>
> **Brentwood Police Department**
>
> **76981 Jones Leavy Drive, 15th Precinct**
>
> **Brentwood TN 37027-1000**
>
> **Cell – 615-776-0900**
>
> **Please call if you need anything. SC**

Anya was elated that Abbey had invited her to such an illustrious event. But then she realized she had nothing to wear, and the event would be at her favorite getaway, Miami. She knew she had to be dressed to the nines, because these galas could be a source for networking and new business opportunities.

Anya retrieved the vacuum cleaner from the hall closet, plugged it in, and began maneuvering the machine across the carpet when something got lodged in the hose. When she reached down to dislodge what appeared to be a piece of paper, she unfolded it, and it was a business card with the name:

There was no reason not to call him now. This was an open invitation. Yes, she did need something. And that was to thank him for the roses and the kindness he had showed her that night. She picked up the phone to dial the number but hung up. She would call once she returned from running her errands and some well-deserved retail therapy.

Cleaning was complete. Anya grabbed her backpack and keys and went down the corridor to the rooftop, where her vehicle was parked. She stopped to take in the city views and the calmness of the Percy Priest Lake. The peacefulness of the lake took her back to when her dad would go fishing and how he talked about one day owning a boat. Tears began to pour from her eyes. How she wished he were here to see her many accomplishments. Especially the one she was standing upon. When her realtor had suggested this property, she had immediately said no, because of the amount of work it would take to get it where she wanted it. But when she came up here, she knew she was home.

She wiped the tears from her cheeks, looked toward heaven, and said, "Daddy, I love and miss you so much. I know you are with me." Anya slid behind the stirring wheel, and off she went.

Downtown was seemingly not busy for a weekday. Anya had gathered the materials for her vision board and journal from Target. While there, she purchased some more cleaning supplies, comforter sets, accessories, and area rugs for the four spare bedrooms. Thank God for the young man who assisted her to her car with her merchandise. She walked to the paint store to select colors that complemented her purchased comforters. She had had no idea how many shades of blues, greens, and purple were out there. After an hour of looking, she gave up and said she would leave this to the experts.

The last stop was to find an elegant gown for the gala. Anya had passed a boutique on her way to the paint store. She entered the establishment and was greeted by a middle-aged woman. Her skin was reminiscent of warm peanut butter. She wore glasses, but her eyes were the color of sand kissed by the sun. And that walk was flawless. It was as if she was a peacock, her head perched high and strutting in all her glory.

When she spoke, Anya could hear a British accent. "Madame, how can I assist you?"

She must have asked the question several times. And when Anya did not answer, she placed her hand on her forearm.

Anya quickly came out of her trance and answered her. "I am so sorry. I know you probably think I must be crazy, but I was taken aback by your beauty."

The woman graciously bowed her head and said, "Thank you."

"I am looking for a gown for a gala."

"OK, is there a particular color you are looking for?"

"No, not really."

"Where is this event taking place?"

"Miami."

"And when is it?"

"In two weeks."

"Come with me," she said. "My name is Margaret Saint Laurent. Please come this way."

They headed to the back of the store. Mrs. Margaret asked her to turn around so she could get a better look at her in the light. After looking at her for about ten minutes, she asked Anya to go to the changing room, and she would bring some gowns to try on.

Mrs. Margaret brought her four gowns, each telling its own story. The first was a full-length black ball gown which she liked, but it was not her. The second was a seafoam green, semiformal cocktail dress; it was nice but not what Anya was looking for. The third dress was an elegant, white, high-split, flare-sleeve maxi dress with a cape; and the last one was a champagne, off-the-shoulder column dress. Anya opted for the last two gowns.

Mrs. Margaret made an appointment for her to come back for some alterations to the length. Anya paid Mrs. Margaret, thanked her for her time, and looked forward to seeing her for their appointment on Friday. Margaret locked the door behind Anya. She could not help but stare, as she looked so much like her daughter Jocelyn, who had run away over thirty years before.

Chapter 7

NOT AGAIN

Royce had just finished a basketball game with his law firm colleagues. He reached for his phone that was in his gym bag and noticed that he had a missed call from Chris, his lawyer. So he pressed the speed dial, and Chris immediately answered the phone.

"Hey, Royce, I just got a call from Bria's lawyer, who advised that she was rushed to the hospital in premature labor."

Royce ran to his car and headed down I-40 en route to the hospital. When he arrived, he was told that she was still in the emergency room and would move to a room in the maternity ward. His mind began to race. Had Bria delivered the baby? If so, would they survive? According to Bria's lawyer, when they had last spoken a month before, she had been twenty weeks. So that would make her about twenty-four weeks pregnant.

The greeter from the front desk tapped Royce on the shoulder to let him know Bria had been moved to her room. She pointed him in the direction of the elevator. He got to the ninth floor and buzzed the intercom. A woman answered, and he said, "My name is Royce Blackmon; I'm here to see Bria Gregory."

She responded, "She is only allowed to have one visitor at a time, and it appears that her husband is at the bedside." As Royce walked away and headed to the elevator, the woman returned on the intercom and told him his name was on a list denying him entrance to the ward. He made his way back downstairs and headed to his car when he overheard a gentleman asking for Bria's room number; he was told that she already had a visitor with her. The man said, "I would love to know who that is because I'm her husband."

Royce got to his car and pulled out his phone. He went to the last text he had received from Bria. The texts read:

BRIA: Baby, last night was amazing. When can we get together again? (AUG 25 10:12A)

ME: Headed out of town for business and will be back in three weeks. I will call you when I land. (AUG 25 11:43A)

The time before that had been July 20. Royce was no obstetrician-gynecologist, but something didn't add up. Especially since today was the twenty-fifth of February

Royce took a deep breath and laid his head on the headrest.

Finally, he had come to grips with the possibility of being a father of a child to a woman he did not love. He even called his parents and siblings to tell them what was happening. The excitement in his mom's voice made his heart melt.

She said, "Royce; this is the first time I have seen a sparkle in your eye since Skylar passed."

Royce could not break her heart. Because he had not told them that the child may or may not be his child.

He drove aimlessly until he decided to park his car and run the trail adjacent to the Percy Priest Lake. Running was something he had picked up after Skylar's death. He placed his BEATS headphones on his ears and began to hit the pavement. His stride was smooth and precise as he felt the calm wind kiss his face and sweat drench his clothes. His heart danced in his chest like a herd of wild horses. All he wanted was for the hurting to stop. He needed his Skylar to tell him that everything was going to be OK. He could distinctly hear a woman's voice saying, "I am here with you, my love." Royce stopped to catch his breath and looked around to see if someone had called out to him. No one else was on the trail but him. He chalked it up to a long and exhausting day and decided to head home.

Once home, Royce climbed into the shower and allowed the wave of hot water to cover his aching body. The thoughts of today's events made him think of the bond he shared with his mother and father. He knew what a devoted father looked like. When Royce had been about six years old, he had been diagnosed with dyslexia. Dyslexia is a learning disorder where people have difficulty reading and interpreting what they read. In Royce's case, he had phonological dyslexia and struggled with processing the sounds of individual letters and syllables, as well as matching them with the written forms.

Royce's pediatrician attributed his dyslexia to being premature. He and his parents spent countless sessions with the speech therapist to help him build his conversational abilities. On the day he was to sit for the bar exam, his dad traveled from Tennessee to Georgia, where Royce was attending Morehouse Law School. His dad was by his side when he took the two-day exam. He remembered his dad saying with tears in his eyes, "Every accomplishment starts with the decision to try. You have beaten all the odds, and now go in there and make your dream of being a lawyer a reality." His constant support over the years is what Royce hoped to be as a father, whether with Bria or someone else.

Royce dried off, dressed, and headed downstairs to review some legal briefs and the spreadsheet from his financial advisor, Brent. He quickly scanned the legal briefs and sent an email to his legal assistant asking that he make the necessary corrections to the attachment, and in addition, that he request an extension for the Jackson case listed on the docket on Friday. Finally, he pulled the notes that Brent had included with the spreadsheet. Brent indicated that he was very impressed with Ms. McMichael's thorough review of the company's financial forecasting. He suggested that Royce schedule a meeting with the two of them. Royce had contemplated whether he should give her a call now but decided against it, as it was nearly eleven. Instead, he would reach out to her tomorrow.

When he dialed Ms. Michael's cell phone the following day, an unfamiliar voice answered. "Activating Excellence

Consulting Firm; this is Stacie; how may I assist you?"

"Hello, Stacie, this is Royce Blackmon; I am sorry; I thought I was calling Ms. McMichael's phone."

"Mr. Blackmon, yes, you are calling her phone. All her calls have been forwarded to the office, as she is on a personal leave of absence."

"Oh, I see. Do you have any idea when she will return?"

"I am not sure."

"Would you be so kind as to let her know that I called?"

Stacie acknowledged Royce and disconnected the line. Royce called Abbey to inquire about Anya. Abbey provided little information other than that she had been home for about a month. Royce asked if she thought it would be OK to send her some flowers. Abbey indicated that every woman loves to be sent flowers and gave him her address.

Chapter 8

No $\mathcal{S}$ANCTUARY

$\mathcal{S}$*ebastián guided his bike* so that it would be parallel to the curve. He removed his helmet, walked to the giant oak tree, and sat under its massive branches. He had arrived at the place he deemed his quiet spot. He had been coming to this exact spot since he was ten—the spot where his life had changed and begun all in one breath. This was the place where he was taught many of his life lessons. This is where he came to seek understanding when things were unclear.

This is where Pop Franklin told him of his son. By then, Sebastián was twenty years old and a junior at Howard University, majoring in criminal justice. Pop and Ma sat him down to tell him they were moving to Nashville. He was excited but scared because he quietly prayed that his mom would return. On the day of the move, they cleared out the spare bedroom, and he noticed a box on the top shelf in the closet.

He reached up to get it down, and the box fell from his grip. Inside there were several photos of a child and a young man. There was either Ma or Pop with this guy in all the pictures. Sebastián was confused; was this a relative he had not met before? Sebastián took the box and gave it to Ma; she began sobbing. Pop had just entered the apartment and saw Ma holding the box. He immediately went to console her.

After Ma was OK, Pop and Sebastián took a ride to the park. They sat under this same oak tree, and he explained that the young man in the photo was his son, Leo Sebastián Franklin.

"Leo joined the Air Force a year after he had graduated high school. He said he wanted to see the world and have the military pay for his college expenses. After basic and advanced military training, he was stationed at Air Force Base Lakenheath in London. Leo was there for over two years, training as a pilot. We were so excited that our boy was seeing the world, and he loved his job as a pilot.

"Leo called one evening to let Ma and me know he was approved for a two-week leave and would bring someone special with him when he came home. Leo said, 'Dad, I need to go, but I will call back after this training exercise and give you my flight itinerary. I love you.' And he told Ma he loved her too.

"Unfortunately, he was involved in a collision with another jet as he attempted to land. Leo was able to eject from the jet but succumbed to his injuries. That day was the worst day of our life. I was so depressed after losing Leo. All I did was work and come home. Soon Jack Daniels and I became the best of friends. Ma had decided that she had had enough and was leaving.

"So when you and Ja'Nae moved into the building when you were eight years old, Ma and I believed that our prayers were answered. God had given us another chance to love another child like we loved Leo. He had given us another Sebastián. When Ja'Nae asked that we take care of you when you were ten, we were elated. Ja'Nae had given Ma all the necessary documents that gave us the legal rights to care for you."

Sebastián remained hopeful that he would see Ja'Nae again. He had gone to the apartment building later that evening, after his talk with Pop, and signed a lease, which he has had for the last seventeen years in his name, just in case she came back looking for him. The last correspondence from Ja'Nae was on his graduation day from college. She had sent a card and a box with no return address to their old address, which had been forwarded. The card read:

My Dearest Son,

I want to tell you how proud I am of you and your accomplishments. You have become such a wonderful young man. Pop and Ma Franklin have done such a great job. I want to tell you that I've been watching you from afar for a long time. I did not want to interfere in your life. I needed to work on myself because I am a broken little girl trying to face a world of uncertainty—a girl who was given a blessing of a sweet boy. I did not want to hinder you from any opportunities that you deserved. One day we will be reunited, and I pray you will forgive me. I love you, and so would your father. You look just like him in your blue suit on graduation.

Enclosed is something for your future from your father.

Love,

JJSL Collins

Four certified cashier checks totaling $750,000 were enclosed in the card. The last photo of Ja'Nae and myself and the brown bear he had as a child were in the box. Over the years, Sebastián had received a birthday card each year and occasionally a Christmas card.

Sebastián did not doubt that his mother loved him and could not imagine what she had gone through, but had she considered his feelings? Did she know how many nights he had stayed up crying with Ma Franklin consoling him in her arms? Or how many times kids would tease him, saying he was an orphan? This story was not all about her.

CHAPTER 9

THE DELIVERY

Stacie had called Anya the day before with one of her weekly updates. How Anya missed and loved her work family. They were why her company was one of the top minority-run consultant firms in the region. Stacie gave her the names of their new clients and those who referred them; they also reviewed the financials to include the net income after taxes for the month.

Lastly, she advised that Royce Blackmon had called on Monday. Anya was surprised, as she had thought he had taken his business elsewhere—especially since their last exchange had been over a month ago.

The intercom buzzed, indicating someone was at the door. Anya was able to see all her visitors on her Ring device. The young lady said, "Hello, I have a delivery for Ms. McMichael." Anya pressed the button on the entry door, allowing her access to the building and elevator.

Anya had received several packages over the last month from family and friends sending their well wishes. She had received some beautiful flowers from her mom and sister the day before. Anya greeted the young lady as she walked off the elevator. In her hand was a vase of assorted roses. Anya asked whether she needed to sign somewhere, acknowledging that she had received them.

She said, "Yes. However, I have more in the van that I still need to bring up."

Anya said, "What? There are more!" Once the last flowers were delivered and placed in her sunroom and living room, she signed, took the confirmation receipt, and gave the young lady a nice tip. Anya could not believe how loved she was. It looked like the botanical gardens had exploded in her house. The sweet smell of the different roses and plants was intoxicating. There was only one note that came with the delivery.

Ms. McMichael,

I heard that you had taken some personal time away. I pray that all is well and that you take the time you need to reignite that beautiful mind of yours. I was not sure what you liked, so I bought them all.

Talk With You Soon,

r/s

R. E. Blackmon, ESQ

Anya was baffled because Royce had hung up on her when they had last spoken. And now he had sent me more than five dozen roses and ten plants; one, she believed, was a miniature tree. She was not sure what was up with him. And how had he gotten her address?

Anya dialed Abbey's number. "Hello, my friend. How are you?"

"I am great."

"What is the story on Royce Blackmon?"

Abbey said, "I am glad you are good. Anya, you sound upset."

"I am not upset Abbey, just a little confused, that is all. I received multiple vases of roses and plants from Royce Blackmon today. The last time I spoke with him, he hung up on me."

Abbey replied, "Royce hung up on you?"

"Well, maybe I was not hung up on. I reviewed a spreadsheet regarding the financial forecast of his start-up company. I gave him my opinion, and he said, 'Ms. McMichael, I believe I have taken up too much of your time. I will consider your suggestion. Have a great rest of your day.' Before I could respond, the line had disconnected."

Abbey was silent for a second. "Girl, he did not hang up on you."

"OK, so tell me the back story on him."

"There is not much to say about Royce. We grew up in the same neighborhood and went to the same school. Royce is several years older than me. I was in a few classes with his younger sister, Logan. I know that he ran with a group of guys who were considered players. But I don't think that Royce was like that. Now his older brother Bryce, on the other hand, was. Royce, for all accounts, was shy and did not talk much.

"However, that changed when he met Skylar Monroe during their junior year. They were inseparable and so much in love. It seemed as if he blossomed overnight. They dated for many years and later married. Sadly, Skylar died in a car accident. I believe they had only been married for a few years. Rumors started circling that he was dating some shady women after she passed.

"I had not seen or spoken with Royce in many years. It was not until we bumped into one another at the gala last year. Before you go and call Stacie and fuzz her out, I was the one who gave Royce your address. He called me on Monday after his call was forwarded to your office. He asked if it would be OK to send you flowers."

After Abbey finished, Anya felt ashamed because she had judged Royce. He was so young to be a widower. She thought about her mom, who had been with her dad for more than forty years before he had passed. The thought of losing someone after being with them for many years was insurmountable. To be able to experience that type of love comes once in a lifetime, and twice if you are lucky. Anya's heart ached for them both. She decided at that moment to reach out not only to Sebastián but to Royce too.

She dialed Sebastián's number, and it went to voicemail. She left a message thanking him for the roses and asked that he call her back once he received the message. Then she called Royce's number, and the message said the number had been disconnected. She called the number again, thinking she had misdialed, but got the same message. Anya thought that was strange. She considered calling Abbey back but did not.

CHAPTER 10

TO BE
$\mathcal{C}$ONTINUED

The night before had been another sleepless night for Anya. She had had another dream, and it was more vivid. Before last night the only thing she could see was a child. This time she saw a silhouette of two people but could not determine if they were men or women. She clearly could hear a child crying and then cooing. She woke up, and for the first time since being home, she had an intense headache but no nausea.

When she had visited Dr. Summerton, the neurologist, he had prescribed some medication for the headaches. He believed that Anya was suffering from severe migraines and not just a headache. Dr. Summerton had suggested that if the migraines continued, he would like her to get an EEG. Anya took the Imitrex as prescribed and went back to sleep. When she awoke for the second time, the pain was gone. She looked at the time, and it was about noon. She had a lunch date with Leah at 1:30 at Poseidon, a new Greek restaurant about two blocks from the office.

Anya arrived about fifteen minutes early and waited at the bar, directly in line with the front door. The bartender asked if she would like something to drink. She wanted a glass of wine but chose a ginger ale since she had just taken medication.

Her phone rang. Thinking it was Leah, Anya said, "You are running late, and can we reschedule?"

The caller said, "No, I would never think to stand you up." This was not Leah, unless she had changed into a man overnight.

He belted out a laugh. "Ms. McMichael, this is Sebastián Collins. I was returning your call."

"Sergeant Collins, my apology. I thought you were my friend Leah."

"It is Sebastián. I remember Leah; we met at your home."

"Yes, that is right, and it's Anya. I was meeting Leah for lunch. She is notorious for rescheduling or being late."

"I am sure she has a good reason."

"She probably does. Sebastián, I wanted to thank you for the roses and the kindness you showed me that night. With the negative press that police officers have been receiving after the killing of George Floyd, Breonna Taylor, and countless others, it is refreshing to know that there are still some good cops out there."

"Anya, you are welcome. I took an oath to serve and protect the citizens of this community. Unfortunately, some cops have taken that oath, which is a privilege, and abused it. I have family members who are also in law enforcement and would agree with your statement. Again, thank you. I hope that you are feeling much better."

"I am; I decided to take some time off and concentrate on Anya. Enough about me. How are you?"

Sebastián took a moment to think about how he should respond. The last few days had been a roller coaster of emotions. He had spent countless hours at his quiet spot reflecting on his mom and his life.

"Sebastián, are you still there?"

"Oh, I am sorry; yes, I have been maintaining."

"That is good. I know your job can take a toll on your psyche."

"That is an understatement," Sebastián said.

Anya asked, "What do you do to free your mind after a long day at work?"

"I like taking Luke out on the road."

"Who is Luke?"

"Luke is my motorcycle."

Oh, I see Anya replied I have always wanted to learn how to ride.

My parents took a couples' course but did not complete it. I have been thinking about taking one myself but have not had the time."

Sebastián said, "You should make time. It's like no other feeling when I am out on the road." I have looked at a few bikes in the past and have an idea of the one wanted but have not decided on one yet. Anya said.

"I can imagine, for now, that I am resigned to my hot baths, a glass of Moscato, and my slow jams playing in the background."

Sebastián's mind flashed back to Anya in her black lace bra.

"Well, guess who decided to show up?"

Sebastián immediately said, "Tell Leah hello. I will let you go so you can do what girlfriends do."

Anya laughed. "I hope this will not be the last time we talk."

"Absolutely not. Why don't you give me a call later so we can continue our conversation?"

"I will. Until next time." Anya hung up and greeted Leah with a hug.

Leah said, "I hope that was not a business call."

"No, it was not. If you must know, it was a personal call."

"Spill it, chick; you are smiling from ear to ear."

"It was Sebastián."

Leah looked confused. "Who is Sebastián?"

"He was the officer you met at my house."

"Oh yes, Sergeant Collins. So he is the Collins that sent you the roses while you were in the hospital. Girl, he is fine as hell. And that body? Make a sista want to go and find his mother and tell her thank you."

Anya said, "Only you would say something like that. But you are so right. I found his business card when I was cleaning. I called to thank him for the roses and for staying with me until the ambulance arrived." Anya did not want to go into what had happened with the shirt debacle or about what she had felt. She quickly changed the flow of the conversation and said, "Girl, let's eat. I am starving.

CHAPTER 11

TO MUCH

Royce walked from the parking garage to his office. He exited the elevator and entered the suite. It was like the first time he had come through the doors. The Italian polished marble floors that spanned the entire office glistened in the sun. The floor-to-ceiling windows framed the grand, hand-carved mahogany desk, complemented by the beautiful abstract art on the wall.

Loren and Stephen looked up from their computers, and he said good morning and headed to his office. When Royce had made partner at thirty, he had been given a choice of offices. He had selected this one for the panoramic views of the city and the beautiful sunsets. He stood at the window reminiscing on the picnic he had shared with Skylar in this office. At the time, there was no furniture here. Skylar called to see if he had eaten, something she regularly did. Royce said no but that he would be heading out soon to grab a sandwich. She said to meet her in his office. Royce was puzzled; he said, "OK, be there in ten minutes. When he opened the door, she had a blanket with candles, rose petals, Dr. Pepper, and a Philly steak with cheese, mushrooms, and onions. That was his comfort food when he was stressed. Royce had a high-profile case coming up, and Skylar knew precisely what to do to ease his mind.

Stephen's voice pulled him from his thoughts. "Good morning again, Mr. Blackmon." Stephen was Royce's legal secretary and had been with him for three years, and he was good. Stephen sat at the round table to review his calendar and the upcoming cases. He reminded Royce to send flowers to his sister Logan for her birthday. "Also, Mr. Jackson tried to call and said he could not reach you."

Shit! He had forgotten that he had had the number disconnected and changed after his last conversation with Bria.

Stephen responded, "I took care of it. I told Mr. Jackson that you lost your phone while out running. I also sent your new number to the other partners."

Stephen was aware of Royce's situation with Bria. They finished their meeting, but Stephen handed him the invitation to the gala before leaving. "Let me know if you plan on attending so I can block your calendar."

Royce made the call to the florist and placed the order for Logan as well as his mother. It had been three days since he had sent Ms. McMichael the assortment of flowers and plants. Was it too much? Did she think he was crazy? Or even a stalker? Damn! He had disconnected the number.

It was 10:00 a.m. Royce dialed Anya's number and held his breath as it rang. It went to voicemail. "Anya, this is Royce Blackmon; I hope that you are well. I lost my phone while running and wanted to ensure you had my new number. When you get the opportunity, give me a call." Royce let out his breath and prayed that she would return his call.

***

Anya thought she heard her phone ring. She stepped out of the shower and retrieved the phone from the counter. There was a missed call from an unknown number. She had emailed Stacie on Wednesday that she would be taking the forward off since most of the calls were from friends and family. Stacie advised that she would send out a mass email to their current clients, notifying them that all communication going forward will be handled by the other consultants until further notice.

Anya had woken up late and had forty-five minutes to get to the boutique for her alteration appointment with Mrs. Margaret. For some strange reason, she did not want to disappoint her. She took one last look at herself in the mirror. The once-dark circles under her eyes had started to fade, and she had put on about seven pounds in all the right places.

She still wasn't sleeping throughout the night, because of

the dreams, and had to take another pill for her headache. Anya made a note to call and schedule an appointment with Eileen and Dr. Summerton. She retrieved her purse, the bottle of Aleve, some water, and a banana and headed out.

CHAPTER 12

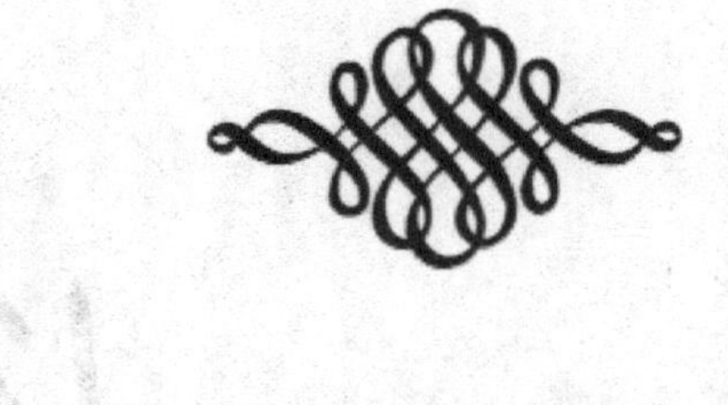

who **A**m i

Sebastián decided to go to the gym for a few hours since he had missed going earlier in the week. He wanted to get there before it was packed. He grabbed his protein drink and a fruit bar and headed to the door. He Facetimed his daughter, Ocean, to map out their plans for the weekend. Ocean answered with the biggest smile on her face. "Hey, Dad!"

"Hello, Princess. Are you up to getting ready for school?"

"No, not yet; we have a two-hour delay this morning."

Sebastián could not help staring at Ocean. She was a combination of Marisa and him. Ocean's eyes were grayish-blue, and her skin tone reminded him of butter pecan, which complemented her heart-shaped face. This morning she wore her hair up in a messy bun just like her mom used to.

"Dad, where are you going this early?"

"I am headed to the gym to work out for a few hours. So, what would you like to do this weekend?"

"Charlie is having her birthday party on Saturday, and I wanted to go. Can we hang out when I get out of school today?"

"That would be fine."

"I can also have Mom drop me off on Sunday, and we can spend the whole day together."

"Sounds like a good plan. What time do you get out of school?"

"At 3:10."

"Ocean, make sure it is OK with your mom."

"I will make sure. See you at four."

Sebastián heard Marisa say "Good morning" to Ocean.

"Tell your mom I said hello. Have a good day at school."

"I will, Dad. I love you."

"I love you too, Princess." They ended their call, and within seconds, Marisa was calling.

"Hello, Marisa."

"Hey, Sebastián. Ocean said you will be picking her up at four today."

"Yes, is that all right?"

"Absolutely! Instead of coming to the house, I have an appointment near you; I can drop Ocean off."

"Thanks, Marisa."

"Any time."

Sebastián was glad that he had such a good relationship coparenting with Marisa. He had had buddies who were not so lucky.

Sebastián had met Marisa Taylor at Howard University during his senior year. Sebastián had sought refuge in the books that he read and the bond that he had built with his brothers on the football team. He loved football and the discipline and teamwork it taught him, but his heart was no longer in it. So when Sebastián decided to tour the campus during his junior year of high school, he was intrigued by the school's history and diversity. The campus was bustling with students hurrying to their next class, and sororities and fraternities were in the yard showcasing their talent through stepping. He knew that this was where he wanted to be.

Even though he had received an entire ride to Fisk University on a football scholarship and other scholarships totaling almost $100,000, Sebastián worked very hard academically and felt he should be able to select where he wanted to attend college. Initially, Ma Franklin was against him going to Howard because she thought it was too far. Also, she was concerned about the environment in which the campus was located. Eventually, after several trips and numerous calls to his academic advisor, she gave him her blessing.

Once Sebastián arrived at Howard University that fall, he was mesmerized by the campus life. His roommate introduced him to several of his friends and the different organizations that were on campus. He had been on campus for four months; as he left his econ class, a classmate handed him a flyer to the multicultural symposium. She said that the seminar and center had helped her as a freshman. Sebastián read the brochure and decided to attend. He returned to the dorm and dropped his books and flyer on the desk. Shortly later, Curtis, his roommate, came in and handed him the flyer. "Hey man, this was on the floor."

"Thanks, I am going to attend the symposium. Do you want to go with me?"

Curtis said, "How do you identify yourself? Black, White, or Mixed?"

Sebastián was confused by his question. "I am Black. Man, are you serious?"

"So you are telling me that both of your parents are Black."

Sebastián really had to think about that. He could honestly say that the topic of race with Ja'Nae, Pop and Ma Franklin never came up. He knew that Pop and Ma were Black. But then he thought about Ja'Nae. She was fair skinned, with hazel eyes. He remembered that the guys would call her "red bone." And, of course, he had no clue who his dad was. Whenever Sebastián asked Ja'Nae, she would say she did not want to talk about it. So he stopped asking.

He called Pop after he left the symposium. Pop answered the phone on the first ring. "Is everything ok, Sebastián?"

"Yes. I have a question I need to ask, and please don't lie to me."

Pop replied, "Sebastián, I promised you I would never do that when you were ten."

"OK, then, what color am I?"

"We knew that the topic of race would come up sooner than later. Especially now that you are at Howard. Where the melting pot has more ingredients than just smoke neckbones. Ma and I always thought you were biracial. But we could not be 100 percent. Ja'Nae was fair skinned, with hazel eyes and blondish-brown hair. We thought your mom was biracial also. Ma said she spoke with your mother and mentioned how her mother would talk about her West African ancestry."

That day changed how Sebastián viewed himself and the world. He now identified as biracial.

Marisa had driven from Atlanta to visit her cousin Rob. Rob happened to be Sebastián's roommate's best friend. When he first laid eyes on her, she sat on the edge of his bed, talking with Curtis. Curtis was president of the National Black Student Union. He and Marisa spoke about the upcoming event the union was sponsoring. Soon the room was packed with other union members as they prepared for their monthly meeting.

After the meeting had concluded, Marisa helped discard the garbage left. Sebastián struck up a conversation about Atlanta. Marisa said she was originally from New York and was attending college at Spellman, majoring in journalism. She wanted to be an international reporter so she would be able to travel the world. Sebastián asked Marisa whether she had considered what she would do if she needed to report a story if a war was to happen. Marisa said with no hesitation that it was a requirement of the job. "I must go where the story is." He and Marisa hung out until that Sunday. They exchanged numbers just before she left. Over the next few months, they talked every day. He saw Marisa again on graduation, as she was there to support her cousin Rob, who was also graduating.

After graduation, Sebastián decided to take a year off and travel. One day he received a call from Marisa, as he typically did. She said she had accepted a job back home at one of the local news stations. She was elated that she was allowed to use the skills she had learned at Spellman, but she wanted to be reporting on a larger platform.

About six months later, she was asked to go to Costa Rica and do a story on the rainforest. Marisa asked if he was interested in going. Sebastián packed his bags and traveled the globe with her. In that time, they learned much about one another and became more than friends.

Marisa had taken an assignment in Thailand, and they were out celebrating her twenty-second birthday. She had complained of nausea and had several episodes of vomiting. They attributed it to being exhausted and the malaria pills she had taken ten days prior. They flew back to the states forty-five days later and found out she was pregnant. Sebastián moved to New York to be closer to Marisa. They rented an apartment on the Upper East Side and prepared for the arrival of Ocean.

They quickly realized that they would be better off as friends than lovers. So when Ocean was two years old, they called it quits. He moved back to Tennessee and regrouped, as he needed to do something different because he was now a father. Several years later, Marisa moved to Tennessee, as they agreed that coparenting would be easier if she were there.

CHAPTER 13

ALTERED PATHS

nya arrived at the boutique with five minutes to spare. Mrs. Margaret was assisting another customer and asked that she take a seat outside the dressing room. She remembered that she had a voicemail from an unknown caller. She went to her saved voicemail messages and entered her PIN, and that smooth baritone voice pierced her ear. Her stomach did somersaults. Anya listened as he explained that he had lost his phone and wanted to ensure she had the new number.

It was not the explanation that made her smile but that he had called her by her first name. Anya was accustomed to him calling her Ms. McMichael. It was something about how Royce said her name. She felt herself starting to perspire. The moistness began to pool between her legs. Anya quickly got up to look for the restroom. Once she located it, she locked the door to regain her composure. Her underwear had become drenched, and she had to remove them. After about five minutes, she heard a knock at the door, and it was Mrs. Margaret.

"Madame, I am ready for you now."

"Ok, I am just about done." She flushed the toilet, splashed water on her face, and returned to the dressing room, where Mrs. Margaret was waiting.

When Anya arrived back in the dressing room, Mrs. Margaret had hung the dresses neatly on the embellished hooks on the wall. The space made Anya feel like a princess: the tailor-stitched white-and-gold linen chair and the ottoman facing the gilt-and-tortoiseshell-inlaid Baroque mirror. The smell of fresh-cut roses filled her nose as she entered the room. Anya placed her belongings on the ottoman and slowly sat on the edge of the chair.

"Would you like something to drink before we get started?"

Anya turned to face Mrs. Margaret. "Yes, ma'am, I would take some water."

She returned with a serving tray with a glass pitcher of water, lemons, and crepes filled with fresh strawberries and blueberries. She placed the tray on the aged console that sat underneath the mirror.

"Anya, how are you?" Mrs. Margaret asked.

"I am OK."

"You look flushed."

Anya became nervous as her face told the story of her earlier event. "I have had some restless nights."

"Have you tried some chamomile tea with vanilla?"

"No, I have not."

"It is what I would give Jocelyn when she could not sleep."

"I will try it tonight. Thanks for the suggestion."

"Let's get started. Go ahead and try on the first gown. Once you are dressed, meet me at the mirror in the viewing area." Mrs. Margaret closed the door behind herself.

Anya began to undress and remembered that she had no undergarments on. She was happy that each gown had a lining to mask her indiscretion. Anya walked to the raised floor in front of the mirror. Mrs. Margaret kneeled in front of her, inserting the pins at the dress's hemline. She retrieved a shoe with ankle laces and a wedge heel from the tower. Anya placed the shoes on so that Mrs. Margaret could gauge whether the length was correct.

"Jocelyn, turn around so I can pin the back." She pinned the sides as well. "How does that feel?" Anya had taken note that Mrs. Margaret had called her Jocelyn.

"It feels good, not too tight."

"The gown looks exquisite on you."

Anya looked at herself in the mirror, and a tear rolled down her cheek. She thought of what it would have been like at her wedding as her dad walked her down the aisle to her future husband.

Mrs. Margaret felt an immediate connection with Anya and embraced her from the back. "Every little girl wants that fairytale wedding. I wished that for Jocelyn."

Anya gently squeezed her hand to show that she felt her pain. "Mrs. Margaret, if I may ask, who is Jocelyn?"

The regal posture that graced this middle-aged woman withered like a rose. She hung her head in defeat and quietly walked to the chairs along the wall in the viewing area. Anya took a seat next to her. Mrs. Margaret raised her head and said, "She was my daughter. Jocelyn is my only child. I have not seen or heard from her in over thirty years. The last time Artisan and I spoke with Jocelyn, it ended in an argument. Jocelyn and I shared such a close bond as she was growing up. Her father was not home much because of his job in the local government. And when Artisan was there, we argued because of his lack of time spent with the family and his expectations of Jocelyn. Artisan treated her as if she was his son.

"We tried for many years to conceive another child. Unfortunately, I was diagnosed with uterine cancer and underwent a complete hysterectomy when Jocelyn was nine. Although Jocelyn excelled in school and did everything to appease her father, it was never enough. Jocelyn completed her secondary studies and was preparing to go off to university when she met an American stationed at the air force base. Jocelyn was in love with this young man. They courted for a year, and he asked her to marry him.

"In my Afro-Caribbean culture, women are said to be headstrong, and Jocelyn was no exception. On the night of the argument, Jocelyn announced at dinner that she was planning to move to the States and marry this young man. My husband forbade her from seeing him. He explained that she was too young and needed to complete her studies.

"I knew what Jocelyn felt because I experienced it with her father. I come from a family that earned their riches in oil. I had pleaded with my father to allow me to attend the university. He finally agreed. This was the first time I had freedom. No bodyguards or round-the-clock servants. I met her father in my second year at the university. We fell in love. My father also forbade the relationship because Artisan is European. I had to choose Artisan or my family. I picked him and was disowned.

"Jocelyn left the dinner table that night very upset with her father. The following day, I went to check on Jocelyn, who was not in her room. On the pillow, there was a note:

My Dearest Parents,

I wanted to tell you that I love you both. My heart is with my love. I would have thought that you both would understand what I feel as you have experienced the same type of love. You have experienced the ache when you are not with that person. Mama, you left your family to be with Papa. Papa, I was never what you wanted. I tried to be the best daughter that a father could wish for. But I was not the son you needed to continue your legacy, and I am sorry.

"I showed the note to Artisan, and he was not concerned. Instead, he said she was upset. 'Give her a few days to cool off, and she will come home.'

"When Jocelyn did not come home that weekend, I immediately drove to the university. I spoke with her roommate, and she advised that Jocelyn had removed all her belongings and told her that she would be continuing her studies in the States. My heart shattered into a million pieces.

"A year later, I received a call from Jocelyn's former roommate, who said she had spoken to her. She said that she was now a mother of a son. Shortly after that call, I received a letter from Jocelyn with no return address. Inside the envelope was a picture of a beautiful baby boy. On the back was the name S. Francis Artisan Collins. That was the last correspondence I received from her."

Anya and Mrs. Margaret's talk lasted for about three hours. Then, finally, Anya knew what it was to speak her truth and release the pent-up hurt. Mrs. Margaret completed the alteration on the last dress and made an appointment for Tuesday at two for her final fitting. This left plenty of time to make additional alterations before the gala on Saturday. Mrs. Margaret hugged Anya and thanked her for listening.

CHAPTER 14

Mis READ

nya stopped at the store to get some items for dinner and the chamomile tea. She was honored that Mrs. Margaret had trusted her enough to share her story. But what made her sad was that she had not seen or heard from her daughter. The pain in her eyes brought tears to her own. Anya gathered the items for dinner and placed the other groceries in the refrigerator. She had a taste for New Orleans–style pasta. Anya put the casserole in the oven, poured a glass of wine, and stepped out on the terrace. She pulled out her phone and waited for the person to answer.

"Hello, Anya, how are you?"

"I am good. How has your day gone?"

"It was uneventful. I am glad that you called."

Anya said, "I did not want you to think that I would not call you back. So tell me about this bike that you have been looking at."

"It is a purple-and-black Kawasaki Ninja 400 with a matching helmet and jacket," Sebastián said.

"What a great choice. I have a Kawasaki too. The 400 is a super lightweight bike and not too intimidating regarding speed. I am not sure about the specs, but I know she is sexy to me."

Sebastián laughed and said, "That is a great way to describe a motorcycle."

Anya replied, "You never heard anyone refer to their bike as sexy?"

"No, I have not."

"Well, Sage is going to be sexy as she glides down the highway."

"So I am safe to say that Sage is the name of your bike?"

"Yes! Maybe Sage and Luke can take a ride together?"

Anya said with a seductive laugh, "That could be arranged."

***

Sebastián heard the doorbell ring and looked down at his watch; it was exactly four. The thing that he loved about Marisa was that she was punctual. He walked a few feet to the door. He opened it, and Ocean greeted him with a hug.

"Hi, Princess."

"Hi, Daddy."

Sebastián asked Anya if he could give her a call back. Anya said, "Sure." The line disconnected.

***

Anya said to herself, *Do not make it more than it is.* She had clearly heard a female voice. Sebastián had called her "Princess." And the female had called him "Daddy." Anya removed the casserole from the oven and poured herself another glass of wine. Why was she concerned with the company that Sergeant Collins kept? It was not as if they were in a relationship. She barely knew who he was, other than he was the officer who responded to a call at her home. But Anya knew it was more than that. Something was going on between them. Or was it only in her mind? Had she misread what had happened that night? Was she just scared of being by herself? Was there something deeper that Anya could not see? Anya finished off the wine and decided to call it a night.

Five hours later, Anya woke up with the urge to pee. She ran to the bathroom just in time. The hot liquid flowed from her body like a fire hydrant in the middle of the summer. Anya sat on the toilet for at least a minute before she finished. She had a headache, more like a hangover. She finally got up, washed her hands, and went to the kitchen. She got a bottle of water from the refrigerator, some Aleve, and made two pieces of toast.

The casserole was still on the top of the stove, along with the empty bottle of wine. She had never consumed a bottle of wine by herself. So, what was really going on? Why had she become upset when she heard a female voice as she talked with Sebastián? Had she become the jealous type? Anya quickly stopped herself from going there. It was a side effect of the wine. She laughed as she held her head and headed back to bed. She would tackle this issue when she was well rested with a clear mind.

CHAPTER 15

UNMARKED

7ERRITORY

Royce was up early and decided to look at the available properties that Brent had sent to him for his new business venture. He still had not heard from Anya. He hoped that she was all right. The house phone rang, which was unusual. It could only be his mother calling.

"Hi, Mom. What are you doing up so early on a Saturday morning?"

"Good morning, son. The ladies from the Magnolia Book Club are meeting for breakfast."

Ella Blackmon was always on the go. Royce remembered growing up and the numerous organizations his mom was a part of. She was the PTA president, assistant tag football coach for Bryce and him, and Girl Scout volunteer for Logan, and she had chaperoned many of the school's dances and field trips. Mom had done this all while she worked full-time as an investment banker.

Royce asked, "What time are you meeting the ladies?"

"Around nine. I was calling to thank you for the beautiful roses. They came yesterday."

"You are welcome. You know you are my first love. Where is Dad?"

"He is upstairs getting dressed to go and pick up Bryce from the airport."

"Oh, I did not know he was visiting. I just talked with him two days ago."

"Sweetie, I got to go. I need to pick up Norma Jean."

"OK, Ma, I love you. Can you tell Dad to have Bryce call me?"

"I will, son."

The list that Brent had sent was extensive. Royce decided he would look at a few today and tackle the others over the next few weekends. He grabbed the insulated thermal mug filled with coffee and headed out the door. The first few properties that Royce viewed with the realtor were not what he was looking for. By the time they had gotten to property number 10, it was one o'clock, the coffee had run out, and he needed something to eat. He and the realtor had made plans to meet again in two weeks.

The last property was about fifteen minutes from downtown Brentwood. Royce parked his car in one of the garages. The last time he had been in Brentwood, he had visited a nice Italian restaurant with clients from the firm. He walked toward the location and thought it would be best to call first. A gentleman answered the phone and advised that there was a forty-five-minute wait. Royce was approaching a quaint coffee shop and decided to go in. The inside resembled an old-fashioned cottage that was in the countryside. He viewed the menu and ordered the vanilla chai tea with 2 percent milk and a scone to go.

Royce looked up, and a beautiful caramel-toned, brown-eyed, five-foot-tall woman exited the restroom and headed his way. He stood behind her waiting on his order. She smelled like lilac and jasmine and wore some black yoga pants that were filled out nicely. Her hair was pulled back in a bun that lay neatly at the nape of her neck. The server called, "Vanilla chamomile tea with a banana nut loaf." The beauty grabbed her order and sat in a booth facing the window.

His order was called, and he strategically sat at the back with a clear view of her. Royce removed his blazer and placed it on the chair next to him. He watched her as she ate the loaf and drank the beverage; it was nothing short of erotic. Royce's body began to react. He stood and went to the restroom

Royce's phone rang. It was his brother Bryce.

"Hi, bro. I did not know you were going to be in Florida."

"Me neither; I am here on business."

Bryce was a land developer and had been instrumental in overseeing many projects that contributed to affordable housing in many cities over the years. Royce asked Bryce if he had any plans for next weekend.

"No, I was going to spend some time with Mom and Dad."

"Cool, I have been invited to attend the annual Minority Entrepreneur and Leadership Gala. I think this would be a great networking opportunity for you. I attended it last year and made some great connections."

Bryce said, "I am in." He was always looking to add some more dineros to the bank.

Royce agreed. "I will send the information later this evening."

"OK."

Royce checked himself in the mirror to make sure that he looked presentable. *Damn*, that woman was naturally gorgeous. She did not have all that makeup splattered all over her face trying to conceal who she was. That was a turn-on for Royce. He left the restroom in hopes that this woman was still there. When he returned to his table, she was no longer there. The chair was empty, but he could still smell the lilac and jasmine fragrance she wore. Royce grabbed his blazer and hurried to the door to see if she was anywhere to be seen. No luck; she was gone. He decided to take a stroll through downtown Brentwood before he headed home.

Chapter 16

RePLAY

Sebastián and Marisa discussed the revised plans for the weekend. They both agreed that Sebastián would drop Ocean off at Charlie's house in the morning, and Marisa would be the one to pick her up. Ocean had come back downstairs from her bedroom when Sebastián and Marisa had ended their conversation outside.

Ocean said, "Dad, who were you talking with when you opened the door?"

Sebastián said, "Why are you asking?"

"Because you had a big smile on your face."

"It was someone that I met at work."

"Is she a cop?"

"No, I had to go to her home on a call."

Ocean looked at Sebastián with a serious expression.

"Ocean, it is not what you think." He shook his head and said, "I will explain it when you get older."

"Seriously, Dad, just be careful."

"So, what do you want to do tonight with your old man?"

Ocean laughed. "You are not old. How about we order some pizza and binge-watch some classic movies?"

"I like that plan." Sebastián was so impressed but never surprised with his daughter. She was constantly expanding her mind by trying and doing new things. He could not take all the credit. Marisa was a phenomenal mom and a great role model for Ocean. Although they had not worked out, they were great parents.

The pizza had arrived, and they both curled up on the couch and selected their first movie. They had nearly finished the third one when Sebastián looked over at Ocean, and she was asleep. He did not want to wake her, so he pulled a blanket from the vintage hope chest Ma had given him as a housewarming gift. He had always admired it. Ma kept all her keepsakes in it. This was where she kept all Sebastián's school photos and artwork, his hair from when Pop first cut it, and the Bible he had received from her when he had gone to Howard. He removed the neatly folded letter from Ma that was in the Bible.

Sebastián,

Although I did not carry you in my womb for nine months, nor do we share the same blood as kin, you are still my son. You came into our lives just when we needed you. Your smile and affectionate laugh illuminated the darkness we felt after losing our own Sebastián. You would always say how grateful you are that we saved your life. But it is you who saved us, and we are eternally grateful.

"Direct your children onto the right path; when they are older, they will not leave it."

NLT PROV. 22:6

Love Ma

Sebastián has always remembered this verse and knew it to be true, as the foundation, guidance, love, and stern talking had been instrumental in who and what he had become. And let us not forget those old fashioned whuppings he received them when he thought he was grown. Pop and Ma had no issue driving to Howard to give him one if he needed it. He knew that he would provide this Bible to Ocean one day. He placed the blanket over Ocean, removed her glasses, and kissed her on her forehead. He stepped out on the front porch and sat on the wooden swing. He dialed Anya's number, and after three rings, she answered.

"Hey, sleepyhead, I am sorry that I woke you up."

Anya said something that Sebastián could not make out. "Good night, Anya. I will give you a call in the morning. Maybe we can take Luke for a ride and look for Sage while we are out."

He released the call and sat looking at the stars that lit up the sky. He could hear Ocean say over and over, "Be careful, Daddy." Sebastián still had no idea if Anya was in a relationship or even wanted to be. They were just having a friendly conversation. No harm in that. He had not been in a serious relationship since Marisa and had dated casually over the years. Sebastián realized the dating scene had changed so much since he and Marisa had been a couple. You had many dating sites to select from, but getting to know the person was virtually impossible. You were unsure if the person in the profile was genuinely who they said they were. He preferred to go back to simpler times when a man picked a woman up, paid for dinner, and escorted her back home afterward. Call him old-fashioned, but he thought it still worked.

CHAPTER 17

FREE AND
BREEZY

Leah called Anya to see what she had planned for today. Anya answered, and Leah could hear music playing in the background.

"Good morning, where are you off to?"

Anya said, "Nowhere; I am at home."

"You sound like you are in a good mood."

"I am. I just left the coffee shop. I also went to a yoga and meditation class that Eileen suggested.

"You have been busy, I see. Do you want to catch a movie tonight?"

"Can I get a raincheck?" Anya asked.

Leah said, "I guess you can, since I am the one who is always asking for one."

"Before you ask, Sebastián is picking me up, and we are going riding."

"And what are we riding?" Leah said, laughing.

"You are so nasty! He has a motorcycle. Today is a nice day to go."

"What time is he picking you up?"

"He said five."

"What are you wearing?" Leah asked.

"I did not know there was a dress code when riding."

"Girl, have I not taught you anything over the years?"

Leah gave specific directions on her attire. "Call me when you get back. I want to hear how it went."

Before hanging up, Anya asked Leah if she wanted to attend the gala. Abbey had called and said she would be one of the cohosts and did not want Anya to be alone at the table.

Leah said yes.

Anya had talked with Sebastián, who cleared up to whom

the female voice belonged. It turned out it was his daughter. Again, she had judged before she could hear his side. She woke up with a slight headache, not a migraine. She had had yet another dream. This time another element was added that freaked her completely out. Her dad was in it, along with three more unknown silhouettes. What were these dreams trying to tell her? After a few minutes, she became calm, and the dream ended.

Anya called and scheduled an appointment with Eileen. Maybe she could shed some light on these dreams. They were becoming more vivid and more frequent. The migraines were tolerable, and nausea had not been an issue for the last few nights, which was a plus.

She had signed up for a beginner's yoga and meditation class. The instructors were great. They were a couple from Belize who had taught this class for twenty years and owned a yoga studio. Anya stuck around to talk with them, and they suggested she also consider seeing Dr. Ahsan, a chiropractor who came to the studio twice a month.

Anya had been thinking about Mrs. Margaret and checked on her. She immediately came out from behind the counter and hugged Anya when she saw her. They chatted for a few minutes until the growling of Anya's stomach interrupted them. The coffee shop was a short walk from her boutique. Anya entered the shop, placed her order, and went to the bathroom. When she returned to the counter, there stood a six-foot, at least two-inch, mocha skinned brotha. He sported a goatee, neatly trimmed, and a fresh haircut. He wore a nice pair of gray slacks with a button-down black shirt that showcased his broad shoulders, chiseled chest, and slim waist. The Italian loafers and lightweight blazer pulled the casual attire altogether. And he smelled like a combination of Calabrian-Bergamot and Ambroxan—intoxicating. She took her order and walked to her usual table that faced the window. Her hips had a little more sway as she slowly took a seat, ensuring that he could see her shapely bottom. She saw him come her way; she lowered her head as if looking in her purse. She occasionally looked around to look at him. The last time she looked, he was no longer there. She waited for about ten minutes, and he never returned. She cleared the table and left.

The ride with Sebastián was exhilarating. He picked Anya up at five, as promised. He graced her door wearing some black acid-washed jeans, a flannel shirt, and cowboy boots. He removed the aviator sunglasses that framed his face. Those eyes put her in a trance. She had to look away; they would not have made it out the door if she had not. She asked Sebastián to come in while she went to get her vest. She could feel him watching her. She took one more look in the mirror before she left. She wore light denim jeans with rips in the knees, an oversized tan cashmere sweater, and tan riding boots. She had let her hair air dry and pulled her natural tight coils up in a sleek bun that lay neatly at her neck. Her lips were lightly polished with a clear lip gloss, and hanging from her ears were a pair of gold hoops.

Sebastián could not take his eyes off her. She was gorgeous. Anya was all woman. How was he going to make it the entire night? He took several deep breaths as he heard Anya walking down the hallway with the vest draped over her arm. Finally, Anya said, "I am ready; lead the way."

Sebastián had taken Anya about thirty minutes outside of

Nashville into Davidson County, to Ashland. The picturesque farmland and winding road allowed Anya to wrap her arms around his muscular body. She laid her head on his back and listened to the beat of his heart. The sound was soothing as the cool breeze swept her into bliss.

Finally, the bike stopped, and Anya raised her head from his back. She removed her helmet, and she was in awe. There stood a beautiful farmhouse in the distance. The house was modest in size, with a two-tone wood-and-stone exterior. The pitched roof and dormer gave the home character. Anya could see horses grazing in an enclosed area. The smell of gardenia and pineapple sage invaded her nose. Sebastián helped Anya from the bike and escorted her to the house's stairs.

The door to the home opened, and an older man greeted them.

"Good evening, Mr. Collins; I hope you had a good ride."

"I did, Mr. Thomas."

Mr. Thomas asked to take Anya's vest and backpack. She glanced over to look at Sebastián. He mouthed, "I will explain later."

No judgment, Anya said to herself. They walked down the corridor into a large formal front room with elevated, exposed wood tray ceilings. The fireplace gave the large room a cozy feel. All the decor was simple and fit the period of the home. Anya sat close to the fire to warm up.

She knew when Leah had suggested these ripped jeans that

it was a mistake. Mr. Thomas had left the room, and only Sebastián and she remained. His back was to her as he looked out the window.

"Anya, before you think that I am some type of drug boss, kingpin, or mobster, I am not. I am a cop and have been for the last twelve years. I purchased this house when I was nineteen years old with money from my mother, whom I had not seen since I was ten. This house was not in this condition when I bought it. It has taken me fifteen years to restore it to what it would have looked like in the late 1800s. Mr. Thomas is not my butler or servant. I hired him because he is a master woodsman. He resides on the property because he was a homeless retired veteran and a recovering addict when we met thirteen years ago. You are the first and only woman that I have brought here. Neither Ocean nor my parents know about it."

Anya's mouth fell open when Sebastián said she was the first and only woman to see the house. She was speechless.

Mr. Thomas was at the door and said dinner was ready. Sebastián was still facing the window. He said, "I will be there in a minute. Mr. Thomas, can you take Anya?"

"Yes, I can."

Anya followed him into the dining room. The walls were covered with reclaimed wood with wrought-iron accents. In the center of the room was a massive pinewood table that sat at least twelve. The smell of barbecue, freshly fried fish, collard greens, cornbread, apple pie, and sweet tea rose from the feast set out on the table. Anya had to pinch herself; she thought she was back at

Big Momma's house eating Sunday dinner with the family.

"Mr. Thomas, you have outdone yourself this time."

Anya looked at Sebastián, and it appeared as if he had been crying. Anya mouthed, "No judgment" and "Thank you."

He mouthed back, "You are welcome."

CHAPTER 18

UNEXPECTED *V*ISITOR

*R*oyce *had been working late nights*, and today would be the same. He still had not spoken to Anya. He was becoming concerned because it had been a week since he sent her flowers. He had briefly talked to Abbey on Monday regarding a legal matter and had inquired about Anya then. Abbey had kept the conversations very brief and said that Anya was still home. Royce considered himself an intelligent man and did not believe Anya had not returned his call because of the roses. Something else was going on with her.

Stephen called over the intercom and said a gentleman was here to see him. Royce looked at his calendar and saw that he had no appointments. Stephen said he had told the gentlemen that he needed to schedule one. But he had been persistent. Royce had Stephen notify security just in case things got out of hand. He walked out to the lobby, and a man sat with his back against the wall. Royce thought he had seen this man somewhere.

The gentleman rose and extended his hand. "I am Nate White, Bria's husband."

Royce shook his hand as a courtesy. He asked if they could talk in private. Royce opted to take the conversation in the boardroom, not his office. The men took a seat at the table.

Royce said, "How can I help you, Mr. White?"

Nate explained that he and Bria had been married for six years. He had met her at a gentlemen's club where she was the bartender. They had dated for two years before they married. Bria had left the club, or so he had thought. Nate said that he was a high-ranking officer in the military and that one of his soldiers had said he saw her at the club stripping.

Royce was confused. "She is pregnant." The last time he heard anything about Bria was over a month ago when Chris had called to tell him she was in the hospital

"Yes, she is," Nate said. "Mr. Blackmon, the baby she is carrying could not be mine. I had a vasectomy right before we met. I had my suspicions that she was cheating. So I had her followed about a year ago, which is how I found out about you."

Nate pulled an envelope from his briefcase. He passed it to Royce, and he pulled several photos out. Royce was in shock. He offered the images back to Nate.

Nate said, "You can keep them just in case you need ammunition in court."

Royce escorted Mr. White out and thanked him for his time. Royce remained in the boardroom contemplating his next move.

***

Anya had a wonderful time with Sebastián. The dinner was mouthwatering, and the conversation flowed well. Sebastián and Mr. Taylor kept her in stitches as they talked about their adventures while remodeling the house. One of the stories told of how Sebastián fell through the roof of the barn and landed in, let us say, fertilizer.

Anya ended up staying overnight because it had rained, and Sebastián was not comfortable riding back. The following day Sebastián cooked breakfast for them. It was nothing like Mr. Thomas's cooking, but the thought counted. True to form, Leah had called to make sure she made it home safely. Anya gave her the details of the night, apart from the information about Sebastián's mother.

The next few days went by so fast. She saw Eileen, and she gave Anya some insight into her dreams, which she was grateful for. Dr. Summerton scheduled her for an EEG in a month. He also prescribed some stronger medication, because the migraines were so severe that she could not get out of bed until Monday evening. Sebastián and Anya talked every day since Saturday. He stopped by on Monday with some soup and kept her company until she fell asleep. He was so attentive and such a gentleman.

Leah came and picked her up to take her to her fitting appointment with Mrs. Margaret at two. They arrived about ten minutes early, so Anya sat outside the dressing room as Leah walked around the boutique, looking at the different garments on the rack. Mrs. Margaret had finished up with her customer and was now ready for her. Mrs. Margaret hung the gowns in the dressing room and placed a pair of shoes there. Anya walked out to the viewing area where she was waiting.

The first gown fit perfectly. She tried on the last one, and it fit equally well. Mrs. Margaret carefully placed each gown in the embroidered garment bag and handed it to her.

"Madame, I enjoyed our time together. Please don't be a stranger. Make sure you take plenty of pictures so that I may see them."

She kissed Anya on both cheeks, and Anya and Leah left. Leah dropped her back at home and went back to work. Anya placed the garment bag in the spare bedroom and went to the kitchen to warm up the soup Sebastián had brought.

Her phone rang. She looked at the number; it did not look familiar. She answered it, because Dr. Summerton's receptionist had advised that someone from the hospital might call if they could get her in sooner.

"Hello, Anya."

Anya's heart immediately dropped to her feet. She took a moment to get herself together.

"Hello, Mr. Blackmon."

"I hope that I am not disturbing you."

"No, you are not."

"How are you feeling?"

"I have had better days, but I will not complain."

"I am sorry that you are not feeling well." Anya could hear the sincerity in his voice. "If I may ask, is there something I can do to help?"

Royce knew she had no family here and wanted to ensure she would be taken care of.

Anya said, "Nothing that Aleve and a good night's rest could not cure. Thank you for asking, Mr. Blackmon. Also, thanks for the beautiful flowers and plant arrangements. The aroma in the house smells fantastic."

"You are welcome. I hope it was not too much."

Anya laughed. "I never thought I would have a personal botanical garden in my sun and living room."

"So I guess you are saying that it was a tad overboard."

"Yes, just a bit."

Royce let out this boisterous laugh that warmed Anya's heart. This was the first time she felt he was letting down his guard.

"Well, Anya, I now know for next time."

"Since you said there would be a next time, Mr. Blackmon, I like any color roses."

"I will keep that in mind, also."

Anya was glad that Royce was more relaxed and did not feel like it was a business call.

Royce did not believe that she had been on personal leave for almost two months and that everything was OK with her. However, he felt that Anya was being vague regarding her health. He made a promise to himself that he would call her more regularly.

CHAPTER 19

NO *J*UDGMENT

Sebastián had ended his shift and was going to give Anya a call when he received a call from Ma.

"Hello, beautiful lady."

Ma, said, "You sure know how to make an old lady feel special."

"Well, it is true. You are gorgeous inside and outside." There was a pause, and Sebastián guessed Ma was blushing. "Is everything OK?"

"Yes, Pop and I are fine."

But Sebastián could detect that something was not right.

"Ma, are you sure everything is OK?"

"There is a letter from Ja'Nae here for you."

Sebastián was speechless. He had not heard from Ja'Nae since he had graduated from college.

Finally, Ma said, "Are you still there?"

"Yes, ma'am. I will be by and pick it up on Friday."

"OK, so I will make sure that I cook your favorites. What time should I expect you?"

"I will be there by six. I will stop by and pick up Ocean so she can ride with me."

"Pop and I would love to see our grandbaby; it has been too long."

"Ma, we were just there on Sunday."

"That is still too long," she said with a laugh.

Ma and Pop had an incredible bond with Ocean. They were the best grandparents a kid could have. Sebastián could only imagine what Ocean was experiencing. She had two sets of grandparents who loved and adored her. Sebastián asked whether there was anything that they needed. Ma said no.

"OK, I will see you on Friday. I love you."

"No judgment!" Sebastián could hear Anya saying. He felt so comfortable talking with her. Their conversations were as if they had known one another for a lifetime. When he had told her about his past, she had listened and heard him. Sebastián felt that there was a connection with Anya that he had not found with no other female. Anya felt comfortable in sharing her life with him too.

Anya had said, "Your situation is somewhat like mine. After I got to the hospital that night, I had a panic attack. I had never experienced a panic attack before. My therapist, Eileen, explained that a traumatic event or stress could bring on a panic attack. Through several sessions, I have discovered that I had not adequately grieved my father's death, which was compounded by the pressure of my job. Releasing the pain and allowing myself to grieve is what I am committed to doing for my mental health. You are lucky."

Sebastián said, "How so?"

"You could have been abandoned in foster care from one family to another. Instead, your mother knew she needed help and put a plan in place when she could no longer care for you. Sebastián, that is what a mother's love is."

It had been sixteen years since he had last heard from her. Sebastián credited Anya for allowing him to see who Ja'Nae was. He could continue to play the victim in this situation or forgive her. Ja'Nae had been a young mother with no guidance. She had done the best that she could with what she had. He was eternally grateful that she had loved him enough to leave him with Ma and Pop. As he had told Ma, he was not opposed to talking with her and slowly building a relationship. He grieved for that young boy at ten and the girl at nineteen who were lost in the world, trying to find their way and survive. However, he was committed to change and moving forward. Sebastián wondered if Ja'Nae was committed to repairing their relationship and what he would do if she were not. *Time heals all wounds, but I am still a work in progress!*

 Chapter 20

*Un*INTENTIONAL

Anya and Leah had finally finished shopping for the gala. Leah found a beautiful gown at the boutique, and Mrs. Margaret was able to make the minor alterations the day before.

Leah asked her how it felt to have two men fighting for her affection. Anya had no clue that this was happening. She had talked with both men. But each conversation was different. She was intrigued by the mystery of Royce. Their discussions were intellectually stimulating. He made her think about achieving the impossible. Sebastián was a protector and wore his heart on his sleeve. He was easygoing and had a free spirit. Anya did not want to lead anyone on. This had never been her intention.

She had genuinely enjoyed the company and conversation of both. They found time for her—something she did not get from Grayson. It had been a one-sided relationship. Anya had poured everything into the relationship for two years, but it had not been enough. He had lied and cheated and made Anya feel like it was her fault. The relationship was toxic, and she had to end it. She took that energy and invested it into the business. This was where she had control and was appreciated and loved for what she gave. No judgment.

Well, at least she thought she had control. Her life was spinning out of control. Anya knew that pain way too well. She needed to be clear on what she wanted and if she was ready and able to give it back in a relationship or as a friend.

Anya was exhausted. She could not wait to get home. She had been at the hospital in the neurological lab for four hours, waiting to get the EEG that Dr. Summerton had ordered. Finally, the tech called Anya back to a secluded, dark room with some soothing music playing. The tech apologized for the long wait. She explained the procedure to Anya and advised her that it should take about an hour to complete. After placing the electrodes on her scalp, she told her to relax and that if she wanted to take a nap, that would be fine. As promised, the test was painless, and she was out after an hour. The tech advised Anya that the final report should be to the doctor by Friday.

Anya made it home, and flowers were waiting at her door. They were from Royce. He had sent a dozen every day since she had told him that she had no preference when it came to color. She needed to talk to them both sooner than later.

It took Anya three hours to decide what to pack for this trip. Unbelievable! She decided to get to bed early. She ran a hot bath and put her slow jams on, and Luther was belting out "If Only for One Night." She submerged her body in the soapy water and closed her eyes. She woke up about an hour later, dried off, and headed to bed. She prayed that the migraines would stay at bay and there would be no dreams, just peaceful sleep.

Anya and Leah had arrived at the airport two hours before their scheduled departure time. Leah was headed to the souvenir shop for a magazine and asked if Anya wanted anything. She said, "A ginger ale would be good."

Anya's phone rang. It was Abbey calling. "Good morning."

Abbey replied, "Yes, it is. I have arranged for a car to pick you and Leah up from the airport and take you to the house. Call me when you arrive."

The agent came over the intercom: "FLIGHT 2365 NONSTOP TO MIAMI, PREPARING TO BOARD AT GATE 4."

CHAPTER 21

MIAMI, ℬABY!

Anya had taken a Benadryl right before she boarded the plane. When she awoke, they were finally descending into Miami International Airport. She and Leah made their way to the baggage claim. They stepped outside, and the humidity was intense. Abbey had said that a driver would be waiting for them when they arrived. Anya spotted their names and walked toward a polished, pearl white 8 Maybach Landaulet. The driver greeted them: "Welcome to beautiful Miami, Ms. McMichael and Ms. Bernard. I am Sal. I will be your driver."

Sal opened the rear door and took their bags. The drive was about twenty minutes. He pulled up to a three-story house with panoramic views of the Atlantic Ocean. Anya could see Abbey standing in the circular driveway. She wore a beautiful gold maxi dress and some leopard-print espadrille sandals. She hugged both Leah and Anya when they got out of the car. Abbey said, "Ladies, enjoy the digs. I will see you later this evening."

Anya asked if she was staying there.

"No, this is for you all. I have a villa about ten minutes from here. A massage therapist will be here at two, and the cook, maid, and driver will be here all weekend." Abbey hugged them again and left.

Leah said, "Abbey is a bad bitch!"

Anya smiled and began walking up the marble stairs to the landing.

Sal had taken their bags into the foyer of the house. Anya was immediately drawn to the floor-to-ceiling windows that magnified the beautiful blue water. She remembered this same view from when she had last been here in Miami. She removed her shoes, stepped on the cool travertine floor, and walked toward the sliding glass door onto the balcony. What a beautiful view. It never would get old. Anya could hear Leah speaking with someone in Spanish. *Damn, I have known her for over ten years and did not know she spoke Spanish.*

"Buenos dias, Señora. Esta una casa hermosa."

The young lady said, *"Gracias. "Qué quieres tomar?"*

"Si, zumo de naranja. Gracias."

"Puedo hacer algo de desayuno."

"Tocino huevos y tostadas."

"Y para la joven?"

"La misma. Por favor."

"Eres muy Bienvenida."

Leah joined Anya on the balcony and sat in the whitewashed wicker chair.

"Girl, you never cease to amaze me. I did not know you spoke Spanish."

"Yes, but I am not fluent. I picked it up when I was dating Santiago."

"Where is Santiago?"

Leah said, "He had to go back to Brazil to care for his mother last time we spoke."

"So, what did you say to the young lady?"

"I asked for orange juice, bacon, eggs, and toast for us."

"Thanks," Anya said, "I am starving."

Leah replied, *"Eres muy bienvenida."*

Anya answered, *"Gracias."*

Leah laughed. The breakfast was delicious as they took in the scenic view and relaxed on the balcony. Once they had finished, Marisol took them to their rooms.

Anya took a short nap and called Abbey. "Hello, girlfriend; this place is straight out of a luxury magazine."

"Yes, it is."

"Thank you again for inviting Leah and me to the gala."

"You don't have to thank me; you are the sister I wished I had."

"Ah, that is so sweet, Abbey. You are like a sister to me too."

Over the last five years, Abbey and Anya had spent a lot of time with each other. Abbey had confided in Anya about some very personal issues. Anya knew Abbey had her back "Girl, I stop it. I cannot ruin this $100 makeup."

On the phone, Abbey was saying to Anya, "The massage therapists should be there within the hour. I have made a reservation for dinner for six at NAOE. Sal will be there at 5:30."

Leah knocked on the door. She came in and sat on the lounge in front of the fireplace. Anya told her about the dinner reservations at six.

"OK, I will be ready," Leah said. "Girl, whoever owns this house is well off."

"Yes, they are. Abbey took care of everything. All we had to do was bring our bags and show up."

"Well, girl, we showed up, and it is time to show out."

"Leah, we are here on business. The gala will allow us to network with other successful entrepreneurs. You know I want to expand the business. I think Miami is where I will be looking to do it."

Leah has no idea Anya had been grooming her to run the next satellite office. This was the reason she had asked Leah to join her here in Miami. Leah had a keen eye for business. And she was a fast learner and a boss like Anya.

Anya wanted to talk with Abbey about partnering together on a joint venture. Abbey had earned her MBA at HEC Paris Business School with a minor in international studies. She had graduated summa cum laude. After graduating, she had been recruited by Berkshire Hathaway. Abbey had decided to venture out three years before and had opened her own financial consulting firm. Abbey had expressed her interest in incorporating insurance concepts into her offerings. Anya would reach back out to Abbey after the gala.

Marisol let them know that the massage therapists had arrived, and they were setting up in the cabana. Anya had already taken a shower and put on the cotton robe left for her in the *en suite* bathroom. Marisol escorted them down a sandy path that led to the beach. Apollo and Drago were there waiting on them. The hour-long Swedish massage and facial was heaven. Apollo had large hands of gold. Anya knew she had gone to sleep with drool dripping from her mouth before he finished.

It was about four, and she went upstairs to unpack. She placed all her toiletries in the bathroom and her undergarments in the armoire that housed the television. She carefully removed the gowns that Mrs. Margaret had packed. Pinned to the inside was a handwritten note from her:

Anya,

You remind me so much of my Jocelyn. I hoped to have given this brooch to her on her wedding day. This brooch is an heirloom that was given to me by my grandmother. When my parents disowned me, she was the only one who refused to stop speaking to me. So she gave it to me on my wedding day. I know you are not getting married, but I think this is an exceptional occasion for you. You are going to be the belle of the ball.

Margaret

Anya had no words. She wished there were something that she could do to help Mrs. Margaret. When she returned home, she was going to go and talk with her about Jocelyn.

Sal arrived at NAOE right at six. Anya chose to wear to dinner the high-split, flare-sleeve, white maxi dress with the cape, six-inch cerulean stilettos, and bangle bracelet with a dangle earring. She wore a twist-out and dazzle glass lip gloss by Mac to accentuate her high cheekbones and mouth. Leah was fierce in a black one-shoulder tuxedo cocktail dress paired with lime accessories and chunky heels. Her hair was pulled into a soft ponytail off to the left of her head.

Abbey was already seated at the table when they arrived, drinking a glass of merlot. She was wearing a burgundy halter top high-wrist form-fitting Egyptian cotton split-leg pantsuit with canary yellow stilettos and accessories. They chose their appetizer, dinner selection, and dessert and ordered their drinks. The food was Japanese cuisine at its finest. The atmosphere was cozy but classy. Anya had the miso soup, *yakitori* with vegetables, and brown rice. She chose the *daigaku imo,* deep-fried sweet potatoes with caramel syrup for dessert. Leah and Abbey chose miso soup, *yakitori* with vegetables and brown rice, and Japanese cheesecake. They were all stuffed and ready to call it a night. They arrived back at the house by nine. Sal took Abbey to her villa, and they planned to meet at noon the next day. Anya said good night to Leah and retired.

CHAPTER 22

GALA READY

Abbey could not meet Anya and Leah at noon because of the changes needed for the gala that night. Anya checked her phone when she got up, and there were no voicemails or missed calls. She was glad there were none so she could mentally prepare for that night. But deep down inside, she hoped that Sebastián or Royce would call. Marisol had prepared an excellent breakfast for them. Afterward, they went swimming and relaxed on the beach for a few hours. Sal picked them up at one and gave them a tour of Miami, starting in the arts district, then to Little Havana, and he wrapped up the time at Bayside Marketplace.

The marketplace is along Miami's waterfront, with over one hundred shops. Anya was able to pick up souvenirs for the girls at work, Mrs. Margaret, Royce, and Sebastián. On the way back to the house, Leah and Sal had sparked up a conversation in Spanish, which Anya did not mind. She was in her little world. She began to think it was selfish to want a man's attention. Did she deserve it? Was she destined to be alone, like Grayson had said when he had left? She needed to pull herself out of this funk. She had less than two hours before the gala.

***

Sebastián had the letter from Ja'Nae in his hand but could not bring himself to open it. Although he was ready to move forward, he was still afraid. He was fearful of disappointment.

Ma pulled him to the side just before leaving the house on Friday. "Sebastián, to face your fears, you must breathe through the pain. You gain strength, courage, and confidence through every experience in which anxiety is evident." He laid the letter on the mantel above the fireplace and walked away.

***

Bryce had picked up Royce from the airport the night before. Royce had called just before boarding and said that Bria was on a rampage. She had come to his office and made a scene, and she had to be escorted off the premises. Before leaving, she had threatened to ruin him financially. That same day he had filed a restraining order against her. Royce knew that Bria had an ulterior motive. After meeting with Nate White, he had hired a private investigator of his own; what he found was beyond unbelievable.

***

Anya was ready and waiting on the terrace for Sal to arrive. She took in the cool breeze and watched as a couple walked hand and hand along the beach. Maybe one day she would be that lucky. Leah called her name; Sal was here. She picked up her head and repeated to herself, *You are worthy and deserve every blessing coming your way.* She slid into the backseat of the car, closing her eyes to relax her unhinged nerves.

Finally, they arrived at the venue. She checked her appearance in the compact mirror she pulled from the vintage clutch purse. The champagne off-the-shoulder column dress complimented Anya's skin tone. She wore an open-toe, lavender, five-inch heel that defined her calf, and the chandelier drop earring framed her face. Her hair was sleeked back in a bun, giving her a sophisticated but regal look. She had opted to keep the lips light with a champagne-tinted lip gloss. The shawl draped around her shoulders was secured by the brooch that Margaret had given her.

Sal pulled up to the Diplomatic Beach Resorts. The views were as breathtaking as those seen from the house's terrace. Anya looked at Leah and said, "Let's go and build our empire."

The Saga Continues...

UNMASK

CALENTHIA MILLER

Preview

Of

Unmask | Book²

UNCOVERING *the* 7RUTH

Anya finds herself between a rock and a hard place. What is she to believe, the word of a pregnant woman or the word of a person she has known for five years who grew up with Royce and knew his history of keeping company with some unsavory women? Trust a man who had no identity until tonight and whom she barely knows? Or take a chance on a person she has spent time with and has grown to admire? Can Anya resolve the issues from her past so that she will find happiness in the future?

***

Accommodating his need to protect and his desire to be good

enough interferes with Sebastián's everyday life. He is stuck in the past. He is unable to resolve the issues stemming from his childhood. He wants to move forward and heal the pain but does not know how to take the necessary steps. Will this turmoil impact his relationship with the people he loves?

***

Royce is a successful attorney who has guarded his heart since losing his wife, Skylar. Trying to mask the pain, he is now potentially trapped having a baby with a woman he doesn't love. Will time reveal the truth and heal his broken heart?

***

Bryce has lived the life of a playboy and is now ready to settle down and be in a monogamous relationship, but he doesn't know if that is possible—until he sits across the table from a beautiful lady at a charity event. Leah is rough around the edges but determined to make it. Her relationship with Anya is closer than a sister's. She doesn't want to disappoint Anya. How far will she go to make her dreams a reality?

Will new relationships blossom out of this chaos and confusion? Only time will tell.

Illustration by Anthony L. Wardrett

About the Author

Unmask is the journey of many faceless women with a story to tell. Their stories are of perseverance in times when those around them gave up on them. A tale of sisterhood, family, and love. It is now time that their voices are heard, expose their truth, and reveal the beauty hidden behind their mask. Dr. Calenthia Miller is a mentor, educator, healthcare administrator, and CEO of Activating Excellence Consulting, LLC, and Canvas of Thoughts, LLC. Calenthia was born to Clarence Miller and Calenthia Johnson in Gary, Indiana. She was raised on the west side of Chicago with her two siblings, Patrice and Leon. Calenthia attended Elizabeth Peabody, Julius Sterling Morton, and Carl Schurz High School, where she excelled and was accepted into the License Practical Nursing Program. While working full-time at Mount Sinai Hospital, she enrolled at Malcolm X. Community

College, where she was awarded the Harold Washington Scholarship. During her time at the college, she was inspired by her English professor Mr. Washington who was impressed with her writing skills, something she had begun exploring when she was about ten. An advocate of learning, Calenthia poured herself into the pages of any book she picked up. She has taken that love of academia and has earned her Bachelor's in Healthcare Management, Master's in Business Administration, and a Doctorate in Healthcare Management with a minor in Leadership. She has also devoted herself to sharing her knowledge as an adjunct professor at several community colleges in Virginia. Calenthia is the proud mother of two handsome sons, Lorenzo Allen, Kahari Bryant, and Mimi, to Armoni Allen. Calenthia currently resides in Durham, North Carolina, where she works as a Health Center Administrator for a notfor-profit organization. Her love for providing service to her community has expanded over thirty-three years. However, in January 2022, while at work, Calenthia suffered a stroke. During her sabbatical from healthcare, she quickly realized that her desire to work tirelessly had masked her ability to recognize and understand that she was stressed. Sadly, this had become her norm. Equipped with that knowledge, she realized her focus would be on her. As a result, Calenthia began writing again to increase her cognitive readiness. Now her time is devoted to what brings her joy: family, friends, traveling, gardening, writing, and good health. Life is too short; enjoy each day as if it was your last, for our Father did not create us to live in fear, chaos, confusion, or stress. Stay tuned, as Calenthia's story is still evolving.

* 9 7 8 1 9 5 3 1 6 3 5 4 7 *